BEYOND

The

BLUE HORIZON

A COLLECTION OF SHORT STORIES # 5

PEGGY MARCEAUX

ISBN: 978-1-956581-94-2

Erin Go Bragh Publishing
Canyon Lake, TX

Manufactured in the United States of America
Book Design by Kathleen's Graphics

Table of Contents

SAVING WHALES WITH MAGIC IN MOBY DICK

SAVING WHALES WITH MAGIC IN MOBY DICK

They call me Ishmail, because I worked for the Postal Service by trade. But, the National Organization of Oceanic and Atmospheric Administration (NOAA) said I should work for a nobler cause. With a hocus-pocus they sent me directly to the time when whales were slaughtered. The hocus-pocus was supposed to put to put me on Nantucket, but it didn't—it put me on nearby New Bedford; I was met there by a fellow quite extraordinary.

He looked me over and couldn't really believe I was wanting to ship out for whales. He told me that whalers usually shipped from Nantucket, but they were shipping from New Bedford this year because of the weather there.

"That's strange," I said. "We are close enough to Nantucket I think I could spit on it."

"T's rough weather;" a local fellow told me. "To take a small boat to the island; of Nantucket from New Bedford. would be suicide."

As a result, I went looking for the nearest boarding house. It turned out the nearest boarding house was the only boarding house in New Bedford.

The proprietor asked me if I wanted "a bed alone or if I'd be willing to share?"

"Well, I'm kinda keen on sleeping alone," I told him.

"The reason I asked is because I have a sareten fella who I think ye wouldn't even know you'd be a-sharing it until ye see him in the marning."

"Really? And what kind of fellow might he be?"

"Oh, he stays pretty much to his self, and it's a large bed. I slept in it one night with a large man, and had plenty of leg room left over."

"Show me this bed," and I could imagine having plenty of room myself.

"I take it. I do so cheaper sharing.?"

"Indeed, it do it would cheaper be. He won't even come into the room until well after midnight." and he kinda smiled.

"Really? Yes, and I tell ye, it will be like just like sleeping alone until ye wake."

"Okay," I said," I'll take you up on that deal."

My next stop, was the café a fella pointed out to me last night, The Spouter Inn. I had pretty much left my back pack in the bedroom. There was nothing in there anyone could want, and brought my bill fold with me. I asked to see the supper menu. They put the breakfast, lunch and supper menus all on one card in front of me. I looked at it, and quickly understood why.

They sold chowder here, both clam and cod. Take my pick. Having tasted neither of them I flipped a coin and ordered clam. I must say that was the best clam I have ever tasted then and for years even after.

I threw my coins down, and then there was nothing to do but go to a Church service, and since I'd be shipping out, and since it seemed I had slept with the devil last night, or someone really close to him, who was tattooed from head to foot, who was hauling a head of a New Zealander by the hair, and a pagan deity he worshiped, it seemed the right thing to do. I opened, the Church door, and there in the back pew I saw him. Queequeg, if I pronounced his name correctly. I had to get that from him because the proprietor was smiling so big I could not get his name from him. And, this Queequeg spoke in such broken English, I didn't know what to make of him.

After the church service, when I came back into the warmth of The Sprouter Inn, he was sitting by the large flame of the fire with his feet on the hearth. There were other sailors in there who paid him no mind, and the reverse was true, as well. After I'd watched him until some time had passed, I noticed he was pretending to read a large volume book, fifty or so pages at a time. Then he'd stop to go "whew," as if it were an ordeal to read that many pages.

My old heart melted. I pulled up a bench close to him and started to share some of what those pages said. You could see the interest grow in him page by page.

After some other chatting, we retired to our room, where he gave me his embalmed head, his little pagan god and, taking thirty pieces of silver from under his tobacco in its pouch, he divided them get in half and gave fifteen to me. When I attempted to do the same, he wouldn't have it. After chatting for a while, we got back in bed and shared smoking his Tomahawk pipe.

I learned he was from a tiny island named Kokovoko. So tiny it isn't on any map. That his father is a High Chief, his uncle is a High Priest, and all his aunts are married to great warriors.

He ran away and decided to take a canoe to Chistiandom to see if they were any better people, but he learned they weren't when he was hired by Sag Harbor to help at the trypots for whalers.

He was given a wheel barrow to take his gear to the ship and invited me to do the same. I took him up on it and put my belongings, and we both were off with the whole town staring at us. The only thing of his he had strapped on was his harpoon.

Once we arrived on board the Pequod, we picked out two hammocks near to each other and unloaded our gear. Having done that, it was just a matter of him picking out a place to put his harpoon. Then it was time to let him in on my secret mission; to save all the whales the Pequod would be chasing, and if I could, Moby Dick.

He looked at me with wide eyes; I think I knew what he was thinking: Then why are we boarding this boat? I wanted to tell him it wasn't that simple. Then I explained the plan, gave him the ideas of the hocus-pocus chant, and told him to keep that a secret until I could tell all the harpooneers.

"I ain't believe dey use it."

"No, I suppose they are more accustomed to the bloody hands they get with the tryworks, but if I offer them the same amount of money, I'll bet they'll take me up on it.'"

"And whut dey do wit the rath of C'apun Ahab.

"That's a good question. They will just have to endure that."

"Now, Queequeg, I need to know the order of harpooneers on the ship. You know, who would Captain Ahab call up fist, who second, etc.?"

"He call me first, den Starbuck's, Ahab's, chef mate's close fren, Tashtebo, a red man from colony west of Martha's Vineyard."

"Then who?"

"Den Stubbs, the se'nd mate who is n'ary seen wit out his pipe, and good humor."

"And harpooneer?"

"His self."

"He does his own harpooning?"

"Don tink he trusts any udder."

"Hmm. That's interesting. Wonder why?"

"One time he say sometin to Ahab 'bout his bone leg makin' so much noise men below can't sleep. Ahab tears into him it a'most makes him cry. After dat, he ain't de same to Ahab.

An' de third is Flask, a short, red face man. Hates whales and hell-bent on killin' 'em all."

"I take it he does his own harpooning?"

"No, Sir, lil Flask has a big black negro name of Daggoo. Flask dun't want to miss one.

Dey are all Isolatoes, cum from islands around,"

"Okay," Ishmail tells him, "The magic chant is," then he goes close to him and whispers in his ear. "Say it as you throw your harpoon."

Queequeg looks down and whispers to himself as if he is trying to remember the chant.

After that the ship started to load up. Ishmail had already met Stubbs, for he slept on the deck of the ship over-night in a tent. All the harpooneers came aboard one by one, and Ishmail could recognize them from the descriptions Queequeg gave him. Then, Starbuck came aboard and went straight to the helm to look over his charts. All that was left was Ahab, who Queequeg told him would come on board just before weighing anchor.

When Queequeg was left to his own thoughts, he worried what the C'apon would think when he missed his whale, that was if the magic chant worked? He knew he'd be in for a string of cursing and feel like the lowest of the men on the boat. If he didn't say the chant, then there was no doubt he'd harpoon the whale, because he staked his reputation on his accuracy.

What a dilemma? What if he lied about saying the chant and it not working? What if, what if, what if?

He asked Ishmail, "Do dis chant work true?"

"If you're asking me all the time, I can say that if it's said when you throw your harpoon, I can tell you, yes," answered Ishmail.

The ship was unusually quite the next day. When you listened closely you knew why.

There would be a footfall then an alternate stump fall. Too, there were some strange foot falls below the deck. In the hold. No one could discern why,

Ah, ha, thought Ishmail, the Captain's on board. He went straight to his stateroom, shut the door, and didn't come out until Starbuck had gotten them into deep water where the whales were. It was a long ride,

"Whale ho!" shouted a shipman. You heard a flurry of feet, including those of Queequeg getting his harpoon, and the alternate of footfall and stump fall of Captain Ahab coming from his room.

"Man the whaleboats!" he shouted! "Queequeg's first!"

Butterflies swarmed in Queequeg's stomach. They had never done that before, he thought. Which should he do? Which should he do?

Good luck, Ishmail said to him as he hurried with his harpoon to the little boat waiting for him.

Queegueg jumped into his whale boat and stood up in the front of it, harpoon above and behind his head, Still, no decision had he made. Then when that huge, beautiful back breached the water, and when its baby calf did likewise, he knew what he had to do: what Ishmail had been preaching all along. Just before he let go the harpoon he chanted "do not break the flesh, set the whale free to live afresh." And just that fast, the cow and calf turned to the right and swam away.

Ishmail smiled wide. Captain Ahab cursed a blue streak. Queequeg!" he shouted, "you've never failed me before! Perhaps I need to move you to the end of the line of my harpooneers."

Queegueg just smiled. "It worked; he told Ishmail. "I ain't belief I ain't seen how bootiful de yar til now."

They asked to see Tashtego next and spoke to him like he absolutely wouldn't believe them.

He said I "already know what beautiful creatures they are, but as long as a white man was going to pay me this much to work in his tryworks, I was certainly going to bloody my hands.

What do you mean you'll pay me the same? What if I want another job?

"Oh, NOAA will keep paying you every whaling season, you have my word."

"You're word, huh?"

"NOAA's word, I can have it put in writing."

"Okay, I take that," he said.

Tashtego was won over easily. He was given the chant, but claimed he didn't need it. He was told to use it anyway to insure he didn't hit the whale by accident.

Tashtego's boat was the next to drop in the water. He grabbed his harpoon. Once the boat was rowed up on the whale, Tashtego raised his harpoon, said "do not break the flesh, set the whale free to live afresh."

The whale made a sudden left turn and was gone. Ahab shouted, "I think I have some form of mutiny on my hands. Damn you, Tashtego, not you, too!"

"Is there no harpooneer who can hit a whale?"

Stubbs was almost last and ready to redeem himself with the captain. Ishmail hurried to him as he was getting his harpoon, Stubbs, just remember they are living, breathing mammals like us. They have a right to live in water as we do in air. And they make the sea so majestic. How can we hunt them for their beauty? Say "do not dare to tear their flesh; set then free and let them live life afresh when you throw your harpoon."

Stubbs thought about what Ishmail had said, and was at the brink of deciding Ahab was after that white whale for vengeance more than meat and ambergris. He decided to follow his heart.

When they threw Stubb's boat in the water, he had to crawl in; he dare not jump. Still, he made his way to the front of the boat where he stood with his harpoon high. Remembering the

Captain's words: *Mast-head, there! Look sharp, all of ye! If ye see a white one split your lungs for him!*

When the whale breached, again with a calf, that's all it took for him to say the chant and miss the whale.

"I'm going to find out what's going on here and damned to all of you missing these whales!" said their Captain.

Ahab began to worry more and more about his men seeing the White Whale. He had a special meeting about it that evening when he walked the deck and said some strange things to his men. Some were even looking at one another thinking he was losing his mind. His mates were the first to notice it earlier, but now it was the entire crew. He was rattling on about not letting Moby Dick get away with taking his leg.

Suddenly Tashtego hollered, "There she blows! There! There! There! She blows!"

"Where-away?"

"On the lee-beam about two miles off! A school of them."

Instantly all was commotion. Flukes came up and went back down. Not only was this a sperm whale, but it was THE sperm whale was in the pod, and Ahab kept reminding his crew they were wasting precious time!

Ahab had gone quite mad by this time. He had planted some stow-aways in the bottom of the ship.

One was a prophet from Japan, who basically assured him he wouldn't die on this voyage seeking his revenge. He simply said he wouldn't be carried off in a coffin. Starbuck was the only mate to stand by him through his delirium.

Draggoo the negro harpooneer was quite forgotten by this time. A huge storm ensued, a typhoon to be exact, with horrendous lightning bolts. In order for the men who participated in

Ishmail's saving of the whales, they had to be saved themselves. Ishmail had to tell them to do that they had to ride lightning bolts back to Nantucket. None were too pleased with that, but Ishmail said I will go first and will meet you on the sand by the sea. Have heart, men. It will work as the chant did. Then he jumped on the next the bolt and disappeared from the Pequod.

That was a hard one for the men to swallow, they only knew they'd be dead as sure as Ahab would not get his revenge, so each followed him. All that was left were Starbuck, Flask, Draggoo, the Japanese prophet and the crew. Starbuck tried his best to convince Ahab not to go Down the path he had chosen. That the White Whale would kill him. With the next lightning bolt Stubbs disappeared from the Pequod.

Starbuck pleaded with Ahab: "Oh, my captain, my captain! –noble heart go not -go not! see it's a brave man that weeps; how great the agony of the persuasion then!"

Never to be convinced otherwise, Ahab ordered his men to "Lower away (his boat)"– he cried, tossing Starbuck's arm from him. "Stand by crew; the prophet proclaimed I wouldn't go out in a coffin."

Ishmail met the believers on Nantucket Beach where they all celebrated being alive and awaited word, if any, from the Pequod. Unfortunately, the Pequod would be rammed by the White Whale. Ahab's walked over to Captain Mathiew working with the rigging on his boat.

"Captain Mathiew, do you have any word from my husband? He was due in some time ago."

"Yes, Ma'am, I did have a gam with him a while back, but I'd say he'd gone quite mad about getting that white whale what got his leg. He said he'd kill it one way or another and asked if I'd seen it. You can see what that whale did to the Pequod there." And he pointed to his left.

He called on Daggoo and his harpoon, but Ishmael and his chant was left to linger in the air and Daggoo missed, too.

"Get out of here!"

"I Ah shall do this myself he shouted," threw his harpoon and hit Moby Dick. Who began to spin and spin around and caught Captain Ahab in its weave.

Down he went with the whale never to surface again, except when he stove the Pequod there. You could see the lifeless captain bound to the ship like another board."

She turned to look at the stoved-up Pequod and screamed.

"Yep," he said. "Done stove her up. I wouldn't be waiting for him if'n I's were you."

"So, how did he die?"

"Way, I hear it his harpoon rope got twisted around that whale and then him, and they went down together."

Ahab's wife turned white as a sheet; she thanked him and walked off. Directly she walked straight into Stubbs.

"Stubb!" she said, surprised. "You didn't go down with the ship?"

"No, Ma'am, as odd as this is gonna sound, that Ishmail fella saved me and a few others what saved the whales. He saved our lives by a white magic."

"By magic?"

"Yes, Ma'am. We did it by riding lightning bolts back."

The End

Skirts Flow Freely over the Seas

Skirts Flow Freely over the Seas

Hiding All Their Wicked Sprees

Though rare, history attests to women crossing the gender gap and appearing in pirate roles, so says the National Geographic Channel. First in the most current date is Rachel Wall from the 1700's. Rachel left her parents' home in Pennsylvania to marry George Wall in Boston during a depression. George had to think for both of them; that's just the way it was. They both went hun every night because George couldn't get a job.

"So," he said, "let's get a fishing boat and try our hands at that?"

That just made them hungrier as they watched all the lobster laden boats chugging by. Then George thought it would be a good idea to let Rachel wave down one of those boats, and, by gun point rob them of just one of those lobster pots, only.one. Of course, the gun would be empty, but Rachel wouldn't have to know that. *She might accidentally shoot herself in the foot*, George thought.

It worked! And, after one more time, they realized what they were missing. The lobster were so good! Then the next time they went out, it worked again, but, they couldn't keep doing that where they were. Wel maybe they could do it just one last time; all Rachel had to do was plug the boat so it wouldn't sink. Oh, but she forgot. So, George had to pull in both her and the boat back out to drain it.

"Rachel, if you want to become a pirate like you say you do, you're going to have to pay attention to detail." George was none too pleased with Rachel. None too pleased at all. He didn't speak to her the rest of the day.

The next day, while they were waiting on lobster boats, and he had simmered down some, a big storm had blown up. It was so bad that a big old swell knocked George out of the boat, and he drowned. Just like that, Rachel's support system was gone forever. She'd continued for week or so, telling people her husband knew she was out here fishing, but that she didn't know what was wrong with her boat. She'd thought about George telling her "Rachel to become a pirate like you told me you did, you have to pay attention to detail." *Why do I think of that when it doesn't help me?* she wondered. She also thought she was pushing her luck hanging around here. She'd decided it was just the right time to embark on her pirate's life now. She would borrow her Mom's eighteen-year-old mare, hitch her to a wagon and head up to Maine. They have lots of lobster there. But she had to lay a little low for now; Rachel wasn't so dumb that she'd be pursued and arrested.

She sat alone in her old, run-down rental, her next home in Maine, and thought of George. "George," she said, "I'm so sorry that happened to you, but it isn't going to change one thing I do. We're going to half everything right down the middle with everything. You'll see. I plan to make you proud of me."

Then she remembered Betsy was still outside and hitched up to the wagon! She hurried low. It wasn't that it was hot out there—it was that Betsy couldn't rest. Rachel unhitched her and out to her. "Oh, Betsy, I'm so sorry for forgetting you." She rubbed her5 muzzle she had hanging walked her to a nearby stable that d clean water and bought her a bale of alfalfa. It was like giving her gold, and Rachel's empty pocket felt it.

"Okay, for that I want to give you a different name. Instead of Betsy, I'll call you, um, how 'bout Valkyrie from my pirate book? Yeah, I like that much better. "How 'bout you, Valkyrie?" The old horse had her head buried in the alfalfa. "Okay, now your fixed for the day, I can go hunting up pirate garb." She left and went home for more money. When she opened the door the ghost of Captain Kidd was waiting on her.

"Captain Kidd? Aren't you a ghost? What are you are here?"

"George asked me to intercede for you."

"Inner seed?"

"No, Rachel. Intercede. It means stepping in on behalf of someone."

"Oh."

"So, what are you up to?"

"I was going to the pirate store to buy me some pirate garb."

"Like what pirate garb?"

"Don't know yet."

She reached in the drawer, got her some money and was on her way out. When she reached the pirate store, Anne Bonny held the door open for her.

"Anne Bonny? A're you still alive."

"No. They caught me in 1782, so I was hanged."

"Does it hurt to be hanged?"

"Depends if you struggle or if it breaks your neck. Anyway, what are you doing here?"

"Don't tell me George asked you to inner seed for me, too?"

"Yes, he did; I think he's worried about you, kid? Does he have any reason to?"

"No. I don't think so. Well, I've got O'Malley and Captain Morgan looking down here, too, to help me out if I need any."

"Really? Then I guess George really is worried. I mean, I've got Captain Kidd over at my--"

"Captain Kidd?" Rachel nodded. "Sorry. Never did like the guy." Bonny cleared her throat. "Anyway, asked Bonny, what are you here to buy?"

"First thing is an eye patch. All my book pirates have eye patches. Then something for my head, like a large bandana. Pirate hats are too expensive and too big. Then I need a cutlass like you and Mary Read had."

They made their way into the store. The proprietor asked her if he could help her with anything, and right away she said, yes, she was looking for an eye patch and a long bandana. He kind of had a silly grin on his face.

"You planning to play pirate?"

She said, "No, I'm planning on becoming a real pirate."

"Oh," he said, cleared his throat and answered with an, "I see."

"Now," she added, "take me to your cutlasses."

On the way there, Bonny told her she shouldn't have told that man she wanted to be a real pirate.

"Why ever not?"

"Because the law can catch you through them that's why not."

"Excuse me, Sir. If the law ever comes looking for me as a pirate, you won't tell the law will you?"

Bonny just rolled her eyes and looked up, supposedly at George. Rachel, who now had a new alias, Abigail Wheeler Barrow, bought one.

"These things are expensive," Rachel noticed.

"Tell you what," he said, "I'll throw in the patch for free."

"If he really liked you, he'd give you the cutlass free."

That bothered Abigail for a long time. Yeh, why didn't he give me the cutlass free?

When they returned to her rental; it was a wreck, so, she apologized for it. She didn't need to introduce the two ghosts who didn't like one another, anyway. She opened George's drawer and told him something about borrowing some money from him for another cutlass that she planned to get tomorrow. Afterward, she turned to Bonny and said "I'm ready to steal my sloop now." And, just like that, Abigail hitched Valkyrie to the wagon, and they were on their way to the quays on the coast. Bonny is telling her all she knows about a sloop and Abigail is wondering if that pirate proprietor will give her that second cutlass for free, too?

When they reached the quay Abigail picked out a simple sloop with a mainsail and jig sail. "Alright," nodded Bonny and got to work. Abigail dropped some alfalfa down to occupy Valkyrie while they worked with the boat. Bonny got in first, showing Abigail where she would sit and how to manage each of the sails. Though Abigail watched intently, the two sails still confused her. Bonny sailed it awhile, then she asked Abigail to sail it for a while back. Abigail started out by going in circles.

Bonny told her to open the second, sail and she'll go straighter. Abigail did that, but instead of going straight, the best she could do was zig-zag. Noticing a lone lobster fisherman in the distance like she did, she started zig-zagging out to him. Once there, he ordered,

"Don't get so close. What do you want, anyway?"

"Just to see if you are getting anything." And she bumped his boat twice.

"Hey, you!"

Oh, damn. "I want to see."

She came around to his stern. Put one foot into his boat, but had one foot stuck in hers. As the waves pulled the boats a part, she was doing the splits over the water. Eventually she fell into it. The man was watching. He kept telling her she had nobody's permission to board his boat. She treaded some cold water for however long it took her to get back into her own boat. But she was persistent and, finally boarded his boat.

"What is it you want, Lady?"

"I want to see your catch."

"There it is, take a look and get the hell outta here."

"Looks like something I can use right now."

"Over my dead body."

She pulled out her cutlass she had in the back of her trousers.

"That can be arranged."

He put both hands up and said, "Take 'em, take 'em. They're not worth dying for."

"Thank you. Don't mind if I do. Now get in that water and start treading."

"Do you know how cold this water is?"

"I think I do. I just crawled out of it, remember?"

Then she got back into her boat, scuttled it, left him treading water and zig-zagged his boat back to the quay. *A guy was standing on the* boarding wharf. He asked Abigail why she took his sloop? Abigail told him it was hers. He showed her his ownership papers, and Abigail showed him hers: a cutlass. When she looked at it carefully, she saw it had a point, so she stabbed the man in the gut. "Those are my papers," she said.

Bonny was waiting for in her in the wagon with Valkyrie, who was scraping the last of the alfalfa from the pathway, when Abigail got into the wagon to head home. Bonny wanted to know everything, and Abigail told her she'd tell her on the way back.

By the time they got back to the rental, Bonny had just finished laughing at Abigail for stabbing that man in the gut.

"But why?" asked Abigail.

"Because with that weapon you can literally chop someone's head off."

Abigail thought about that all the way back to town.

"Well, she said, anyway, I need a change of hair dye, and then we need to leave Maine. When she went to get the red dye, she heard the scuttle butt that a man was found treading this cold water here in Maine and was picked up by the marine police." *Maybe I'll go back to Boston. There's lobster there, too. and Cod, and no marine police, I hope*, she thought.

"But, if you get caught in Boston you'll be hanged," said Bonny,

Abigail never heard any of that. She wondered if that proprietor would give her a second cutlass for free.

Back home, at the rental, when Abigail told Captain Kidd that she stabbed that man in the gut with her cutlass who wanted her sloop, a laugh come down from the heavens.

"Goodness. Who is that?" she asked Bonny.

"Grace O'Malley," Bonny answered.

"Is no one up there on my side?"

"Yes," said Captain Kidd. "George is."

"Oh, my faithful George."

She stewed up the lobster this time with a hot sauce. She'd been thinking about changing her name to Peggy Sue and having their new schooner named the Peggy Sue and George, too. What do you think about that, George? Hmm? She turned the peeled lobster over. With onions and picante sauce, it smelled wonderful. The next day, after she packed up her cheap pirate novels, and hid both her and George's money in her shirt, she said I have two stops to make before I'm ready to get out of here.

She went right to her drawer, took out the piece of paper folded up with George's cut in it, and stuffed in in her shirt. Bonny and Kidd just looked at one another as though Abigail was a little touched in the head. Bonny and Kidd thought it really odd, since the guy was dead, but that was really her business. Still, she remembered that she, her horse and wagon got home a bit shaken, but the butterflies kept her good company, and she smiled. *To think I could make that kind of a difference in life in someone's life,* she thought.

I can name our boat the *Peggy Sue and George, Too*, and take on the new alias. Abigail had to go. When she got back home, she told Bonny, hoping Kidd wouldn't follow. She left the place like it was, but took the cash for George, and stashed a novel or two in her pockets. She traded in her wagon for another, but kept her old horse, Betsy, renamed Valkyrie.

"Come on Bonny," she invited, "we'll go to Boston after one more time here."

"You be careful in that state. They'll hang you as sure as you think you're free there."

Peggy Sue just ignored the comment. "Well, first," she said, "we need to start looking for another quay."

Bonny volunteered to sail *The Peggy Sue and George, Too,* to Massachusetts for her, but she wanted one more chance to get something from this State.

"Thank you," and with that response Peggy Sue started looking at quays there after this last Chance.

They looked all around. The coast was clear, so Bonny pulled the little sloop around to the boarding wharf, worked the sails where Peggy Sue joined her. "I can look for a slip in Martha's Vineyard," she said to Bonny and "start scouting around Cape Cod. Maybe find someone with a pot filled with lobster or cod. Cod would be a nice change for supper."

She had to borrow some of George's money to rent a slip in Martha's Vineyard when they arrived, plus they had to paint the new name on the sloop. She thought, *George, I'm sorry, hon', I'll pay you back with interest; I'm just looking for our next sucker. I'm sorry I cut my hair off, but I've done it for a disguise so we can be successful. I dyed my hair red. I know you don't like redheads, but I think people have now seen me as everything but a redhead. I hope you like the name of our boat: The Peggy Sue and George, Too. I had to take that alias and give up Abigail. So, I became Peggy Sue*

LeDieu. Think you can live with George LeDieu, hunh? Love you, babe.

The next day she found her "sucker." He was fishing for lobster off the northern coast of Gloucester. She backed her boat out of the quay, with all her trusty pirate paraphernalia, turned it around and started zig-zagging toward him. She was unaware she was zig-zagging, though, and wondered if a storm was brewing.

The mariner in the distance had heard by mouth about the approach of a vessel that almost drowned him, and how it seemed to zig-zag. He was ready for her, but not for that hilarious patch and the "Arrghh" that came out of her mouth. She had her head covered and everything. He couldn't help but laugh.

"What's so funny?" she asked.

"That ridiculous eye patch," he said, when he could stop laughing.

She actually got her feelings hurt. "What's the matter with my patch?"

She pulled out her hanger. "Does this look like I'm playing pirates?"

"Yes, it does," he said, by this time laughing hysterically. She near tried to take his head off by chopping at his neck. She didn't see anyone watching as she looked around the area. Oh, the butterflies, the butterflies! It was something she wanted to feel again and again, and she did seven at her own peril.

She decided it was time to buy a small gun. She already had Valkyrie hitched up and ready to go. She first went in and stole several bales of hay from the feed store; that got her a thumbs O'Malley's voice came laughing from the he

But she grabbed the new cutlass, a pair of pirate's high boots and absconded from the store with the proprietor grabbing the back of his neck and screaming "Help!" at the top of his lungs.

O'Malley's laughter stayed with her all the way to Boston. Bonny accompanied her all the way there. People looked at her and wondered who Peggy Sue was talking to.

"Yes, I hit him on the back of the neck because you told me I could chop a man's head off."

"Oh, Abigail, don't you know how to use a cutlass, with all those pirate novels you read? A cutlass is used to slash someone's throat."

"Well, that would have made matters simpler if I had known that at the beginning."

"And what's this talk of you wanting a schooner? Last I heard it was a sloop?"

"That was before I knew I couldn't sail one. If you have so many ghosts up there. Why can't I have my own ghost ship? It'll be great fun for all of you sailing again on the high seas in my pinky schooner."

"Hmmm. Never thought of it that way." Peggy Sue was so proud of herself for coming up with an idea. "Well, that 'll never fly with Rackham and Kidd. Can't put two male captains together. Just doesn't work."

"Fine, then, it'll be you, me, O'Malley and Read."

"First order of business is to find a schooner, then get something to eat. We passed a *Blackbeard's Seared Cod and Breakfast* back a couple of miles, and I'm sure Valkyrie is both hungry and thirsty, too."

"No. First order of business is to find a gun store," said Bonny. "I want you fully protected if you ever encounter a gun. Best thing around is a blunderbuss, as long as you don't blow your right boot off."

"C'mon, Bonny, don't write me off as a total nincompoop."

Some more laughter from the heavens.

"Would you kindly tell that woman to stop laughing at me."

"You tell her."

"Stop!!!" Peggy Sue yelled up.

They found a gun shop, picked her out a nice-looking blunderbuss, and because, they didn't want to get into trouble their first day there, they bought it rather than stole it. The shooting range would have to wait until after supper.

Peggy Sue insisted on not scrimping in regards to Valkyrie. She paid the feed-store farrier to unload the alfalfa, give her a freshly mucked stall with clean water, and to both clean out her feet and to nail some new shoes on her. Of course, it went without saying that she deserved a fresh bale of alfalfa after that long trip, and one every day from that day forward until they were through in Boston. She also told him that, if anything ever happened to her, to send Valkyrie home to Jeff and Betsy Wilson in Philadelphia, Pennsylvania. She gave him ample fare.

After supper it was down to the range where the targets were only twenty-five yards away.

"Think you can hit that?" Bonny asked Peggy Sue.

"Of course." Peggy Sue slipped the blunderbuss from its scabbard on her right hip, tried to take aim with the unwieldy firearm, and blasted a bullet from it. It missed the whole target.

"Reload and try again," Bonny prompted her.

This went on for some time, with Peggy Sue missing every time.

More laughter from above. The gun got heavier and heavier every time Peggy Sue had to aim it.

"Could you do this and prove to me we don't have a defective gun?"

"Sure. Just reload, please."

Bonny took a shot and hit the target almost dead center. "You just need to hit the target somewhere to get a kill shot. These things are not accurate. They're just noisy and scary to the people being shot at, but it's the best we have so far."

Peggy Sue said, "On to find my Pinky Schooner."

"Well now, Peggy Sue, we need to wait a bit and watch what comes in to port. If there is another Pinky

Schooner, I'd say okay. If there isn't, your Pinky will stand out and make you an easier target."

"Then what would you recommend?"

"Then I'd recommend just a small schooner. That way there is no waiting to it."

"Okay, I'm ready to just get this done. I've got Valkyrie all taken care of and the days are limited until I have to come back and see to her. Have you cleared it with the women ghosts?"

"Yep, they are all on board." (excuse the pun)

"Great. Let's go get our schooner."

And, so, they went to the docks and wondered who owned what. "Oh, heck," said Peggy Sue, "let's just take one."

That's just what they did. Peggy Sue was then introduced to Grace O'Malley and Mary Read, who wasn't quite herself since she lost the baby.

"Okay, welcome aboard the *Peggy Sue and George, Too,*" she told them. "I can't quite wrap my head around a ghostly crew."

"A ghostly crew," said O'Malley. "I'm no crewman; I'm your Captain. *You're* part of the crew."

"But, it's my schooner."

"I'm no crew member. I lead or I'm out."

It was a hard pill to swallow, but swallow Peggy Sue did. O'Malley started barking orders, and the others complied. The sails were unfurled, and off the schooner went. The object was to rob every ship they came across on the high seas of money. Money, money, money. Peggy Sue and George would split everything right down the middle. She had their money folded in her shirt.

Their first encounter was with another schooner that was out for a pleasure voyage. The *Peggy Sue and George, Too,* blocked their forward passage. All it took was showing them her hangers. Then Peggy Sue jumped on board and demanded cash from the all the travelers. She got it, then jumped back on board her schooner. Their next victim was a trading schooner traveling to Boston to bring distilled liquor. Again, she jumped on board that boat, and robbed it of all the cash the captain had. Her third victim was a sloop heading for Gloucester, robbed the crew of all their money, then, again, jumped back on *The Peggy Sue and George, Too*, and was on her way. This went on for weeks before someone pulled a gun on Peggy Sue; the only human on board was forced her to pull out her blunderbuss. She shot a big hole in the schooner. It starting taking on water badly, and Peggy Sue had no idea what to do next. The ghosts disappeared on her. She had to bail out in a lifeboat with only a paddle.

"Bonny? What do I do now?"

Nothing. She heard nothing.

She was found guilty of plundering on the high seas and robbery, for killing a man and assaulting others, found guilty and sentenced to hanging by the neck until dead, which by the neck until dead, which happened on October 8th, 1789. George was by her side holding her hand; a bag was placed over her head, and the trap door opened. She felt George squeeze her hand just before her neck snapped. When she opened her eyes again, George's ghost was right there with her.

Now we get to be together for eternity, he said.

Yes, I think so, he answered.

"I don't think I am, and I wish I could have Valkyrie with me. I wished I hadn't left her.

Arrgghh

Another woman, Jeanne de Clisson, was a prolific French pirate in the mid14[th] century she appeared on the high seas chasing French ships, both avenging Olivier IV her husband's death, and further his having to first endure unspeakable torture for a crime he did not commit, Her hulls were painted black and her sails red to reinforce her anger with the King for killing her traitor, though he did die opposing the king in the war against Breton 's throne. Jeanne's husband convicted of treason by way of letter and sentenced to be beheaded. *"Mon Dieiu!"* she stayed afloat with two of her sons, Guillaume and *said, not (torture aussi?)* The English did manage to engage her flagship and sink it, but she and two of her younger sons Oliveri V and Guilliam managed to stay afloat on boara0ds 1 they were picked u0 be Bretons. Unfortunately, her youngest son died exposure before Jeanne and Olivier V was rescued.

That didn't deter her. She and her younger sons and another floated on boards in the sea until Guillaume died of exposure. (Attend Giumell contentirm, Tu ne puex pasr pasarreter maintenant les Bretons vont tellement traverse une rage totsale devant le gibet) she told him. "The Breton's will soon come to our rescue. You can't quit now. Papa is going through complete outrage before the Gibbet," she told Guillaume right before he took his last breath, but they did save her other child afloat with her. She continued pirating, killing every Frenchman who came into the English Channel, leaving only one man alive to let the King know it was she who attacked them. She would hide out among the many islands in the Channel, waiting on her next victim.

After her husband's death, many of the nobility were angry because they thought it was an unjust death for a nobleman. She'd even took two of her boys to see their father's head on a pike. That only made the piracy go on for another thirteen years. They never caught her. Eventually, she retired in France near *Chartres,* the home town of Napolean's *General Françios Severin Marçeau,* whose funeral is depicted on the *Arc de Triphome.*

La Fin

Another pair led more complicated lives as pirates. They started as newly met friends on Jack Rackham's pirate ship, a sloop he stole from Charles Vane, named Ranger, He took lover a while before named Anne Bonny from another man, but didn't marry her, since he had already stolen her as wife to a man, named Johnson.

Then, Mary Read was captured as part of the booty from Johnson. But what was it? A man? A woman? Mary had a sad back story. Mary married. a man in the service who was killed in a war. She grieved and that grief dulled her skills for fighting, but that's' just what she wanted to do now as a pirate when Jack Rackham captured her. She disguised herself as a man, and. that's what the crew thought she was because she had her long red hair hidden under her tricorn hat. Anne was really taken with her, so she showed her true self to Anne. It didn't matter to Anne, so it was presumed they became lovers.

Anyway, Jack Rackham, Calico Jack as he was as known because he dressed in calico often, and did not like Anne and Mary's relationship, but because they were the best pirates on board the ship, he couldn't do much about it. So, it went on for months, as did the piracy. Mary left her hat off her head and let her red hair flow as she put the sword to her enemies. They often bared their breasts to their enemies to show their defiance of societal law. She and Anne seemed to draw strength from the other, fighting alongside one each other, always received equal bounty to the men when the fighting was over, with no complaints from the men. That was honest equality.

"So, Anne, where are you going to hide your booty? It's more than we've ever gotten before."

"Same old place. Mary. No one's ever bothered my knickers; can't see them bothering with them today."

"Then I'm going to do the same," and then she took her latch key, unlocked her chest and put the booty in there.

"The ship is going in to port," said Anne, "let's find a tavern and get a brew."

"Yeah, buddy," Mary answered.

After about a mug each, they were feeling pretty good, and felt unable to hold their feelings for one another back. They started to make unmistakable eye contact that expressed their intimacy. A pirate, another clientele member, walked out, saw them and said, "get a room," which they did after one more beer so they could talk more openly. Mary said, "You know I hate the way Frank Trundle looks at us."

"Really? How does he look at us?"

"Snooty—like. Like we are beneath him; just raises the hair on my arms."

"Really? Mary, we can take care of that easily."

"We can?"

"Yep. When he isn't paying attention to one of us during a boarded fight, the other one goes behind him and, slash, cuts his throat open; it's that simple."

"Oh, I like that idea," said Mary.

Before too long there was banging on their door the likes of which they haven't heard before. When Anne shouted "who is it," the banging just resumed.

"C'mon outta there, Anne," boomed the drunken voice of Captain Jack.

"Want do ya want? Anne dared to ask."

"I want to see my wife if neither of you mind."

"Well we do," answered Mary.

"You stay outta this, or I'll cut your throat."

"Over my dead body!" exclaimed Anne. "And I'm not you're wife!"

"Well, if that's what it'll take. You're either coming out now or I'm going in to get you." Anne jumped up and put a chair against the door handle to lock him out. That only made him furious. His ruckus at the door angered the other customers, which got Captain Jack thrown out. On the way lout he shouted, "I have more rights to you than that whore in there!"

"That's it," said Anne. "He can insult me, but he has no right to insult you. She put her robe on and went to remove the chair from the door, but Mary stopped her. "Let's have one evening to ourselves before we have to swing in our hammocks with the men."

There would normally be hell to pay on the morrow with one exception: both Anne and Mary were much fiercer swordsmen than Captain Jack, so the drunken, loud mouth would back down sooner than the cutlasses. It also helped tremendously that both Anne, and especially Mary, were agile and light could work their way up the rigging with no difficulties. They didn't complain when it was time to scrub the deck and clean up in the kitchen, either. They were sweethearts in every other way but literal sweethearts to Captain Jack. That was bound to get under his skin, and finally it did.

On the very day he was going to get rid of Mary, a terrible storm blew up in the Atlantic around Nassau. Since they had no weather warning device, they weren't ready for it. The swells were tremendous, lifting the ship up, then sending it surging when it broached hard, knocking everyone on board to the deck who wasn't braced. Jack needed the main sail and genoa sails furled deeply, and the storm jib and trysails unfurled.

Captain Jack hollered through the wind. "Mary, get up there. You and Anne are the only ones I know that are that sure-footed."

"I'll go, Sir," Anne said, respectfully.

"No," he shouted back, you may fall. She can do it better than anyone." *Besides she may fall and take care of my problem,* he thought.

At one point Mary was hanging by one hand, the wind was blowing so hard, but she was getting the work done. Anne never took her eyes off of her. "Hang on," she hollered up to Mary

Finally, what had to be deployed was deployed, and what had to be unfurled was unfurled. He had to give her credit; she was the best he'd ever seen. Then the ship; started to yaw and Captain Jack decided at this time all he could do was ride it out. So, he had his bosun (boatswain) blow his whistle for crew to pipe down (go below, pull down, unwrap the hammocks and turn in.).

Some of the green horns on the ship couldn't stand being below. They retched and had to come on deck seeking some relief. All they found were others retching as well; some made it to the galley's side;

others just had to retch where they stood. It was altogether a discouraging sound and smell to both Anne and Mary who knew they had to scrub the deck when the storm had run its course.

When it had run its course, and when the crew got the ship turned back around. when the ladies were almost finished scrubbing the deck, when Captain Jack, looked all around with his spyglass and hollered, "I see booty off the starboard side. Good for the hold." When he got his bearings, he realized he was near the Jamaican coast. He was sitting at the Bahamas but the storm had, in fact thrown them a good way there. At which time everyone shifted gears and prepared to board a ship in Nassau for a fight.

"Let's go with that little sloop William. It looks fast."

Mary and Anne grabbed their hangers (cutlasses) while others favored their sabers. Hangers were much easier to wield in a ship. There were no such things as special vests that could deflect the blow of a weapon; only the skill of the weapon wielder, how fast he/she was, or how he/she could predict his/her opponent's next move could protect them. At one point both Anne and Mary were standing side by side, exacting the same exchange of banging hangers as the other.

45

Directly, Anne was cut. That made her angry, and she went after the man with wild eyes. Next thing you know Anne stabbed him in the gut; he lay in anguish for a bit rolling from side to side, then he lay perfectly still, dead, on the deck. The fighting continued all around him until no one was fighting an enemy except Anne and Mary. There was no quit in them.as lo as an enemy lived, When the enemy lay all dead, then it was time to tend to the slashes and stabs of the Ranger crew before they could divide the booty.

Calico Jack, Anne and Mary continued to pirate the ships up and down the coasts around until they arrived at Bry Harbour Bay in Jamaica. It was there that Jonathan Barnet had set a trap for the pirates that the crew of Calico Jack's blundered into. It was October, 1790, that the pirate—hunter hauled them all in. The men were sentenced to death. And, whether by hook or crook, the women had managed to get **themselves** pregnant, and the law would not execute a pregnant woman. Mary felt something was wrong with her pregnancy, so she refused to leave the jail cell, but they let Ann walk right out. To this It was known that Mary Read died in jail, likely of something related to her pregnancy in 1700.

Almost The End

Finally, there was the case of Grace O'Malley, an Irish woman who took over the clan after her father's death. She inherited land, horses, and a fleet of ships, all at the expense of her brothers. She was a good leader and marauded ships up and down the coast of West Ireland. She got in trouble with Queen Elzabeth I when she started plundering too close to England who was already concerned about her taking away what she believed to be English money and goods. Elizabeth decided to end that by kidnapping her son and nephew, and demanded she come, herself to beg for their release.

When she came, she started off poorly by refusing to bow to the queen and by blowing her nose in a noble man's handkerchief and then throwing it in the fire. She won the releases of her son and nephew, but went on with her piracy until her death in 1603, the same date as the Queen. She won their release either by showing a quiet compassion for the Queen who was suffering with a mouth full of bad teeth, or by getting out of there when the Queen was tiring of company. Like Elizabeth I, she died in 1603, presumably of old age.

Her Irish name was Grainne O'Maille, daughter of Eoghan Dubhdara O Maille from Umhaill, Ireland and commander of the O'Maille Dynasty and the White Seahorse.

The End

Peggy Marceaux

Praying with Polish Salt Mines

Praying With Salt
from the Polish Salt Mines

Part I.

Olgierd woke at 4:00 in the morning to the cacophony of kitchen utensils, pots, and pans: Anna's making gruel and dark, coarse bread for his breakfast. He would pull himself up, still tired from working all day long yesterday and most of the night at the salt mines. He went outside relieve himself, came back into the house and stepped into the kitchen.

"Dorby (morning)," he told Anna in Polish and then kissed her cheek. She placed him a mug of near beer on the table as she reached in the oven for the pan of dark bread. "You're not going to return to that lantern job again today, are you?" she asked.

"Anna, the money is too good to refuse it." Anna simply turned her back on hi

continued to stir the porridge, mixing in some of last night's ham and cabbage.

"I just want my husband to come home tonight," she said aloud. He pulled a wad of

bread from the loaf and assured her he would. "Hunh," she shrugged his assurance off.

"Saying it won't make it so." After eating his breakfast, he patted her on the butt, grabbed his lunch bag, stuffed his mouth with bread, and was careful not to slam the door on his way out and wake the children.

He met his friend, Boleslaw Plazynski, outside to walk to the mine. Just southwest of Krakow's city center, in a grassy and unassuming valley, a town sat, called Wieliczka with an amazing salt mine. In 1844, Olgierd and Boleslaw hurried to the direction of it and prepared to take the 1,073—foot staircase down to one of the 178-mile horizontal passages. Olgierd knew Segfried would be waiting there with the Grant Wheats' lamp for him. The lamp was new in those days. Every man who agreed to use it, staked his life on the walk down the passage being a success. The miner using it had to be sure to crawl on his knees to stay low below the methane gas and rely only on its tiny flame to get where he was going. That's why the money was so good—too good for Olgierd to turn down. Olgierd made it down passage four just fine. He struggled a bit going down passage five because the methane was stronger there. He wouldn't turn back, though, and eventually reached the end of the passage before waving a red flag to warn Segfried it wasn't safe enough for anyone else to go on at that point. After swinging the pick axe for a while, the two men were relieved when the lunch bell sounded. It was too strenuous for the men to just talk leisurely swinging a pick axe.

"So, you did okay with the lantern?" asked Boleslaw?

"Yes, mercifully," Olgierd said while he crossed himself. "I don't look forward to you ever having to do that."

"You don't ever need to worry about that with me."

"I hope not," Olgierd answered, relieved.

Then they got busy on their fun and most enjoyable exercise: praying with salt, Olgierd with his Black Madonna, and Boleslaw with his altar top.

"Just put it out of your mind because I'm not," Boleslaw told him. The fifteen minutes they gave themselves to wolf their lunch own came quickly before they it wanted to.

They hurried to eat to get to the most enjoyable part of their lunch break: praying with salt, Olgierd's Black Madonna and Boleslaw's altar. Olgierd was finishing off Madonna's left shoulder and Boleslaw the right corner of the altar's table top.

"So, what's going on with you at work tomorrow, Boleslaw?"

"Now, don't get upset about this, but I'm carrying the Grant Wheat's Lamp down Passage 2."

"But, Boleslaw, you just told me you weren't going to this, then you turn right around and do it."

"I had put myself in a quandary about telling you at all, I guess."

"Please, rethink it," begged Olgierd.

The hair on his on his neck stood up. "I thought I didn't need to worry about you carrying it.

"You don't."

"You do know the key to successfully carrying it to the end is to stay on your knees below the flame, don't you?"

"I know how to carry it, Olgierd. I don't need anyone to tell me what to do with it." Olgierd stopped giving him advice and hoped he knew what he was talking about. He didn't want to overstep himself and challenge his friend's knowledge or masculinity.

Part 2

He told his wife, Anna, about it when he got in bed that night. She turned to him, put her arm around him and said, "As long as it's not you."

He whispered, "I couldn't live with myself if something happened to Boleslaw. He has five kids to feed and his wife would be devastated." The next morning came soon than Olgierd wanted it to. He walked to the mines with Boleslaw, but reluctance walked hand and hand with him.

"I'll see you at lunch," said Boleslaw. "Have to walk Passage 2 with the Grant Wheat's Lantern first."

"Best of luck," said Olgierd as he walked away. Stay low the whole time." Olgierd just couldn't help himself; he just had to warn him. Right before lunchtime there was a huge blast. Men were scurrying to find protection from salt blocks falling down from above and away from the walls. Olgierd got a sick feeling. Boleslaw had done something wrong. He just knew it. All they found of him was his wedding ring. They supposed it could be his wedding ring, anyway. They asked Olgierd to inform his wife and return the ring to her. He took a deep breath. It was a big ask, but he agreed, knowing he was his closest friend. He went home first and told his wife.

"You know we'll have to help them out, he told her.

"Do we have some extra clothes for the children?"

"I don't know. I suppose I could scrounge some up Poor Ariadna. I really feel for her."

"And you know we'll have to cook for them, too. For a while, anyway,"

"I'll start with borscht (beet soup with cabbage, potatoes, oxtail, beef, carrots, etc.). I can cook that up fast."

"I'll start with the bad news, the clothes, and then tell her we're bringing supper."

"You want me to go with you to give her the bad news?"

"Nah, I think this is something I need to do myself." "

"Just don't fault Boleslaw anything."

"Though I would love to, I wouldn't do that."

Olgierd knocked on her door.

She answered. "Oh. Mr. Liwoski, please come in. I wasn't expecting to see you at this time. Are you and Anna doing well?"

"Oh, yes, ma'am we are. I'm afraid there was an explosion at the mine."

She pulled up a chair for her to sit, afraid the news pertained particularly to her. Already her children were starting to come out of their rooms.

"We heard that," Ariadna said. "The Grants Wheat's lantern."

"Yes, Ma'am," and he handed her what remained of Boleslaw. She doubled over and nearly passed out.

Olgierd caught her and let her cry until her crying was done for now. "We're thinking ahead and sewing you some clothes and making you a good meal for supper. So, please don't worry about chores for the rest of the day, or week, for that matter."

Ariadna was in a stupor during that time. All she could do was kneel and say her rosary, walk to the nearby church and pray for strength. Since her children started at eighteen, they were old enough to cook and did an admirable job under the circumstances. Anna stayed at the sewing machine most of that time and had whipped up some crinoline, a long gown with sleeve less tunics along with stockings and wimples to cover girls' hair. All in all, they made their mother's heartache as gentle as it could be.

Part 3

Meanwhile Olgierd was lonely walking to Wielieczka. He didn't look forward to the day. He had no idea that Siegfried was preparing to ask him to carry the Grant Wheat's lamp that day until he could find another man. Olgierd wouldn't do it until he told his wife, so he hurriedly walked home instead of eating lunch. As one might imagine, he left her in shambles about it, and hurried back.

But, Olgierd had a smart head about him and made the passage just fine. Just one, though, because the fumes got to him in the next. They heard no explosion, so all was well, at least. The next day was Sunday, and Anna insisted they go to Mass, in light of what had happened to Boleslaw, and the suffering of his family. The family all put on their church clothes to make the 10 AM service. Father Pardieu (the Catholic Church rotated its priests and nuns to keep them from developing intimate relationships, ergo the different nationalities); stepped out of the sacristy with his liturgical vestments, an amice, an alb, a cincture, stole and a chasuble. Each carried a meaning of its own.

He started the Mass with the benediction: "Dominus vobiscum" (The Lord be with you) followed by the congregations' reply" et cum spiritu tou (and the spirit be with you). Then comes a quick In Domine Patris., et Fili, et Spiritus Santi. Amen. Where you made the sign of the cross because you'd just been blessed. Then the Mass progressed as usual. Olgierd passed up communion because he'd failed to go to confession in a while, so his son felt he could do the same. Anna looked up at Olgierd who just shrugged his shoulders. After Mass, Olgierd kept hearing a young man crying behind him. It was Bartel. The oldest son of Boleslaw. His entire family was behind them. Olgierd got up and slid in beside Bartek.

He put his arm around the boy. "You know," he said, "it's a terrible thing to lose a father, but it's even more terrible for a wife, young daughters and young sons. You're the oldest boy," said Olgierd, "which means you need to step up to become the man of the family now. Crying doesn't become a man of the family."

"But I'm not ready to do that now."

one of us know when we'll be called to lead; only God knows, and he springs it on us when we least expect it."

"What does that mean, 'the man of the family'?"

"Well, it means you'll have to find a job and support your family. Let's see. Your seventeen, right? I think I could get you a job at the salt mines where your Papa worked." Ariadna interrupted her rosary an looked up at him. He looked over at her. "Oh, no worries. I can guarantee he won't be carrying the Grant Wheat's Lantern."

And the only way he can guarantee that is if he carries it himself, thought Anna, a bit distressed."

"I'd enjoy walking with you to work like I did with you Papa, sack lunches in hand, wolfing down our bread and small ale the first fifteen minutes so we could work on chiseling out our holy images the last 30 minutes. Me on the Black Madonna, and your Papa finishing up his altar in the third chapel. He was never allowed to finish it, Bartek."

"I'll finish it up for him. How would the pay be?" Smart boy, thought Olgierd. Thinking about the money. It's relatively good money for a peasants' salary, but the hours are long.

"You're a strong boy; the hours shouldn't affect you much."

"Okay, I'd love to follow in my Papa's shoes. When do start?"

"Don't you want to talk it over with your Mama first?"

"As the man of the house, I feel I can make my own decisions." Ariadna looked abashed and defeated.

"Well, we'll know as soon as I get the okay form the mine's owner." Anna turned around in her pe.

"I insist he speak to his Mama about it first."

"That would be the respectful thing to do," Olgierd agreed. "I think your Papa would want you to get your Mama's blessing." Anna turned back around and smiled. We always work together better as a team.

The okay came quickly and Bartek was walking to the mines by Wednesday. And, just like Olgierd had said, he met Barek outside at 5:00 with his paper lunch bag, eager to see what his Papa had been working on.

"There'll be a good deal of breaking away rock salt most of the day," Olgierd told Bartek. "That's where the back-breaking labor comes in. We remove chunks of salt and put it in a wheel barrel that we haul away to a wagon." But, Bartek was strong and not afraid of the physical labor. In fact, after seventeen years of living at home, and doing mostly women's work, he invited it. His two brothers, Piotr and Borys, though much younger, envied and admired him. When he entered the mines and walked down all those stairs to the third chapel, he was awe struck. He had no idea his Papa was so talented.

"I don't know if I could finish this altar after all. I am at a loss for words to know how he even got this far."

"You wait for the Lord to inspire you," Olgierd said.

"Do you do that for the Black Madonna, too?" "Most definitely. The Lord had to inspire me for everything, even for carrying the Grant Wheats' Lantern."

"Maybe that's what my Papa did wrong. He didn't wait to get inspired."

"No. What your Papa did wrong was he didn't stay on his knees for the whole passage."

"Why was that important?"

"He allowed the tiny flame to detonate the methane gas floating above him." Bartek was quiet for a moment, thinking.

"But it was an accident, wasn't it?"

"Of course it was an accident, Bartek. He wouldn't have purposely left you and your family without a Papa."

After that, they returned to the pick axe work of removing the salt rock from the mine. Soon, the lunch bell sounded and the men hurried to retrieve their sack lunches. Bartek and Olgierd sat where Bartek's Papa used to sit with his friend, and hurriedly ate their cheese and brown coarse bread. They swallowed it down with jars of small beer.

Afterward, they went to take up where they each had left off with their holy sculptures. Bartek took in the entire tabernacle of where the altar was placed. He was beside himself about where he should begin. Then it occurred to him to say a small prayer for inspiration. Suddenly, a eureka moment came to him. He knew where to begin and how to continue. When Olgierd checked on him, he smiled, then returned to his Blac

Later that night, after walking Bartek home, his sister, Agata, stopped Olgierd and told him to thank Mrs. Liwoski for her effort and kindness, but she had the cooking down now.

"In fact, she had been cooking up a recipe of podpolomyki (oldest known recipe for Slavic flat bread cooked on an open flame.) for Bartek to take to work tomorrow; indeed, she wanted to invite the Liwoski's for dinner on the weekend. She's having all the dishes the Pole's loved: pierogi (dumplings); bigos (hunter's stew) golabki (stuffed cabbage) kotlet schabowry (pork cutlet); barszez (traditional red beet soup); zurek (sour rye soup severed with sausage); kielbasa (smoked and seasoned sausage); and mizeria (polish cucumber salad)."

"Wow!" exclaimed Olgierd. "Please let us contribute and bring some of this for you," Olgierd insisted. "You're doing so much work."

"No, it's our way of thanking you for your support and for taking care of Bartek."

"Now, understand, this is only me saying 'okay'. You'll have to get my wife to go along with you, too."

She smiled a beautiful smile. Only a woman can smile like that who is soon to be a bride, a smile of utter happiness. She brandished a ring on her right hand he hadn't seen before.

"Oh," he took her hand and admired it. "Do I know him?"

"Tomasz Kowalski," she didn't look him in the eyes a bit embarrassed as fit her situation.

"Oh, the Kowalski's? I've heard of them. Congratulations. Maybe you can have him over during your Zakaski so we can get to know him better." She just grinned that big, beautiful grin, nodded and kept on working.

When he got back home, he shared what he learned with Anna.

"Oh, Olgierd," she said. "Where are they going to get the money for a wedding?"

"I told her I didn't think it was a question I should ask her."

"Thank you." "Let's propose it during the Zakaski (invitational meal)," she suggested.

"You're right. It should come from me." He smiled at her.

"Good idea. But let's agree now how much and where it'll come from," he said.

"Of course, Kochanie (baby, honey, sweety). Absolutely," she put her hand on his cheek. "I just think that's the least we can do for Boleslaw and Ariadna. I can't help me think that that could have so easily been our family."

"Not so easily. You never had much faith in my abilities with that Grans Wheats' Lantern. I told you I was very careful with it though I'd lost lots of friends to it."

"I don't want to argue with you about it, but I think I was as responsible for your success as you were." He was reaching in the cabinet for a glass, but hurriedly turned on her, "You?"

"Yes," he said. "Soon as you left for work eat day you were going to carry it; I was saying a rosary to the Black Madonna." He fell in the kitchen chair nearest him.

"Oh, Anna, I didn't want you to worry so for me. I tried to work so carefully that you wouldn't have to."

"And thanks to us, I didn't have to," she said smiling. He walked over to her and put his arms around her. "I juthat Boleslaw could still put his arms around his wife" "Oh, Holy Jesus, I do, too, Olgierd."

Part 4

Pt. IV: The night of the Zakaski came quickly for Olgierd; working eighteen-hour shifts was catching up to his age. He and Anna waited until later in life to have their family, which was different to most couples in the 1800's. That helped them have more money than most, which allowed for them to give Boleslaw's family a decent wedding.

Still, Olgierd was feeling the effects of staying up late in the night; he sure wasn't looking forward to having to drink vodka at a wedding. When they were greeted at the door, Ariadna said, "Czesc (pronounced CHESH-tch) greetings and witamy (welcome)." The aroma was overwhelming.

"Czesc to you and yours," responded Anna. "My, but this house smells sooo good," she said. Anna, who was known as a good seamstresss , was dressed smartly in a colorful long jumper dress of dark green with red flowers in the skirt, a red vest with ornate flowers in pink and gold over an off-white, long sleeved blouse' its hands and collar were covered by a delicate lace.

"Wow! I can't wait to sink my teeth into all of it," said Olgierd. Anna elbowed him.

"But, you will," she said, looking disapprovingly at him.

"Oh, of course I will." Olgikerd had more of the Krakow look, plain, while cotton pants, a heavily decorated vest over a white cotton long-sleeved blouse and high black boots. Both he and his wife had forgone headwear until the wedding. But they had the children dressed well. Antoni in long black, cotton pants, black moccasins and a long-sleeve white shirts with a black, yellow, green and red vest, and a red sash for a belt. Bronya wore a green flowery skirt with pink poppies, a cute Krahow vest covering a three-quarte-length sleeve, white, cotton blouse, and she even sported a white apron. They were the picture of the eighteen-century Polish peasant family, par excellence.

When they entered the home there was no remnants of sadness teft from the past. Everything was joy and completely given over to rebirth. Olgierd walked directly up to Tomasz and introduced himself, with a hardy handshake, like he was the reincarnation of Boleslaw, himself.

After a scrumptious and long evening of great food and drink, Anna told the women they had to let her do the dishes and seat themselves at the table with Olgierd—that she'd join them in a bit. Thay were all confused, as anyone would guess, but did what they were told. "

Alright now have you two figured out a date for your wedding?" Tomasz took the lead.

"Yes, Sir. We wanted it to be on Boleslaw's birthday." At that, Olgierd bowed his head, then whipped his eyes. Anna heard him and hurried to Olgierd. She came over to hug her husband

"He wasn't expecting that,". Anna told them. Olgierd sighed heavily and then carried on.

"Well, Anna and I would love to pay for this wedding."

You could hear all the air get sucked out of the room. Ariadna put her hands over her face and started sobbing, Anna, again, wiped her hands and came to her rescue. Tomasz stood up and said,

"Now, Mr. Liwoski, I'm not broke. Sit yourself down, Tomasz, and hear me out. I never claimed you were broke. By paying for your wedding what we want to do is buy you a couple of pigs for food, then some land to build your house on, pay for the festivities afterward and, finally, the bride's wedding dress. There's plenty more for you to pay for."

Thanks to Agata, Tomasz calmed down and was thankful for all Olgierd and Anna thought of that they had not. Soon Ariadna had stopped sobbing and was pulling Anna's hands out of the dish water.

"How can I thank you two enough for all you've done for us? And even so, you continue to do more? Boleslaw and I were truly blessed getting to know you and your family," Ariadna shook her head.

"We were both blessed getting to know one another," Anna told her, yet again wiping soap from her hands. "Now, if you would do me the honor by letting me sew Agata's wedding dress, and yours as well." Ariadna knew what a wonderful seamstress Anna was and was taken aback by her generosity. "Please let Agata and I pay for the material." "Absolutely not. Giving a gift doesn't work that way."

So, after all the sewing was complete, and after the ground was broken for the couple's new home, and after the pigs were sent for slaughter Oprepare fiid fir the meat and the festivities, and after the holy water was sprinkled on the ground of the new home, and after the vows were said, Agata and Tomasz on Boleslaw's birthday, the Idses of March, 1850, attended by their family and friend they weren't soon to forget.

As a finishing touch, Anna and Olgierd left them a card that said Gratulacje! (Congratulations!) Wszstkiego najlepszego! (All the best!) Iside was a sum of roubles. Agata shared the roubles with her Mama along with a picture of Boleslaw's chapel that Bartek had finished. Olgierd offered to take Agata, Tomasz, Anna, Ariadna, her children and their children down there to show them in person. He asked them to come up with a time. After that, neither Anna nor Olgierd felt they had anything left to give Boleslaw, outside of demonstrating to his family that hope can be borne from their loss.

The End

Ripped From the Headlines

Peruvian Man Lost at Sea 95 days

Ripped From the Headlines
Peruvian Man Lost at Sea 95 days

Maximo Nappa, a fisherman from Peru, decided to go fishing on his day off. The weather looked good and his boat was in good repair. He asked his grand Maw-Maw for two weeks-worth of sandwiches just in case he needed them. The only thing is he had to take the boat down the on a 300-foot on a drop; from his home in the canyon of Machu Pichu to the shore line of the beach. But, today was his day to fish, so he was up to it. He stopped on the way down and bought some: salt water shrimp and some mullet to cut up, then he was ready to go.

He put the boat in the water not too far from his entrance to the shore line. He grabbed everything out of the truck, form the life jacket to his hat, to the bag of two-weeks-worth -sandwiches he ask his grand Maw-Maw to prepare for him for this trip. He had mixed feelings, because he knew he'd miss seeing his baby niece.

He pull -started the motor and it purred just like the day he brought it home from shop, the promise of a good day of fishing. His first catch brought him luck. It was a really big fish bur it was a tuna no less. His grand Maw-Maw's favorite fish! He could hear her ooo and ahh over the taste of its freshness. He decided to throw a piece of mullet out a little deeper. What he got he wasn't sure only that it bent his pole in half. When he could get it up enough to see it, he saw it was a shark. He wanted no part of that, so he cut the line. He threw the head of the mullet threw farther out. Again, when he least expected it, it hit. This time it pulled him and his little boat out to sea.

By this time a storm was brewing in the distance. What happened to my beautiful weather? he thought. It started to rain. He carefully unfolded the sandwiches and started to eat. He always found himself ravenous when he was on the water. He brought some sardines and Vienna sausages to augment the sandwiches, which he ran out of quicker than he could reasonably believe. After seven days the coast became a large expanse of sand. He didn't recognize where he put the boat in, therefore, he wouldn't recognize where to take it out except to say he thought he recognized his truck. He thought, anyway, if he had the gas in his motor. He almost got swamped a couple times where he had to use his motor to save himself.

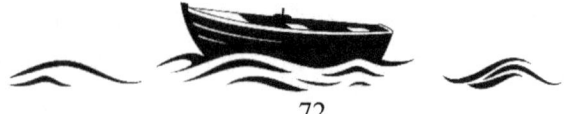

On the thirtieth day, Maximo was completely out of food. He was hoping for another food source and cursing himself for letting the shark go. That's when he noticed them. The Cock roaches; they were swarming the inside of Maximo's boat. He knew desperate people ate them, but, was he desperate enough? He decided he was and started catching them one by one and popping them into his mouth. Crunchy. Very crunchy, but he thought they bore no nutritional value at all.

Besides, all that popping and crunching was done in no time at all, and certainly didn't serve to stave off his hunger. He pulled his belt in to the third hole then was on the hunt for something more substantial to put in his belly. He did have the head of a fish left for bait, but it was a bit soggy from being fished a whole day without a bite, so he was wary of using it again. Still, it was all he had for bait, so he was going to use it. He spit on it as superstitious people were to do, and threw it back in. Monetarily, something started to pull on it. Whatever it was straightened the line tight. He felt it. It felt much like a crab when it wouldn't let go of the line. He pulled up to find a heavy turtle on it. He was elated. A turtle! I can eat that! And he started to work his way into the turtle with his knife.

When his knife wasn't busy cleaning fish or turtle to eat, he was etching another day on the hull of the boat. This was day number 44. He ate the turtle raw. of course, and was always looking for the next food source. Since he was clean lout of shrimp and mullet, he had to look up to the sky. Maybe a bird will fly down here. Directly, the next day, and albatross came to sit on his prow. My, God, he thought, are my prayers being answered? He watched it carefully, afraid to scare it away. When it came back again, he developed a plan.

He took some fishing line and made a noose for its foot, then extended the line into the boat and locked it in place a ways down. Finally, he put the end of it in his own hand so he could pull the bird tight when it tried to fly away. And the next morning, sure enough, the albatross came back as if to say, here I am, take me. And that's just what Maximo did. He trapped the bird, and was so ravenous, ate it all, feathers, eyeballs, beak, all of it. He used the shell of the turtle to collect rain water, or drank the blood of the turtle at times when there was no rain.

Afterward he marked down 50 days. He was starving by the time the Ecuadorian patrol found him. A helicopter came bay calling his name: "Gaton, a boat is coming for you. Hang on." It was the next day the Ecuadorian patrol and his brother found him on day 95.

The End

Flying to Freedom

Flying to Freedom

Eduardo and Armando had grown up miserable under Castro's oppression in Cuba. They dreamed of escaping it. As young boys, 16 and 17, their only escape had been playing baseball when they weren't working the cotton fields in Betancourt, a sugar cane village in the Province of Matanzas. Armando was promised welding lessons when he was there, but that never happened. Instead, they plotted for months what they could do with no dinero. They came up with a daring ploy that may have cost Eduardo his life. They decided it was a go anyway.

They went to the airport one night to check on the runways and the one flight they'd agreed to take. They waited in the tall grass for the jet to approach them and then jumped out at the last minute to look up into the wheel wells. They wanted to see if there was enough room for them to fit in each one. There wasn't much, but decided it was worth the risk. They would be back the next evening with rubber-soled shoes, cotton for their ears and a rope to tie themselves in.

Armando never told his parents, his four brothers or one sister, nor Maria Esther, his girlfriend, though he would miss walking her on the seawall at night. As for his family, he was so poor he was tired of rationing food and living in a single room. He was going to America via Spain so he could become an artist. He could live with his uncle in New Jersey. He was sure his uncle would see to him becoming an artist. They let you be anything you want to be in America.

The night had finally arrived, and the boys had an odd mix of nerves and butterflies. Eduardo chose the right wheel well and Amando the left. They watched the jet come taxing down the runway right at them, then pause to turn around. Both boys took off together without a sound. They raced toward their wheel wells, grabbed hold of struts and pulled themselves up. Armando found that he had to stuff his 5'4", 140-pound body around the hard structures that wouldn't give an inch. When the wheels started to close, they pushed tightly against him so he couldn't breathe. He thought he might be crushed. Then, to his surprise, the wells opened again, showing him yet more room at the top, which he scooted into. He had no idea of knowing that the captain had radioed the Tower he seemed to have one wheel hatch not close as it should, so he'd open it and close it again to make sure there was no major malfunction. Nor had he known that was probably the time Eduardo either fell to his death, or had fallen into the hands of Castro's prison guards

The rest of the trip can only be surmised from the cabin and pilot conversation. There were 147 passengers and a crew of 10. Captain Valentin Vara del Rey, 44, had settled in to his routine flight of eight hours and twenty minutes, going 170 mph. The temp outside was -42 below zero, but the cabin was a snug 76 pressurized degrees. All was well, he thought. When he arrived at Madrid's Barajas Airport, walked down the ramp from the cockpit, and awaited the car that would take the crew to the Airport, a soft plop fell to the ground near them. They were stunned. José Rocca, the security guard was the first to reach Armando.

"His clothes are stiff as a board."

Captain Vara del Rey kept mumbling, "Impossible. That's impossible."

When they called for an ambulance, that's what the medics said, too, yet, here was Armando, asking if he were in Spain.

"Yes, young man, you are. You certainly are," a nurse told him. He suffered nothing worse than frostbite for all that. But needed bed rest for near a month. He had lots of letters, mostly from free countries, and from his uncle in America, lots of phone calls. His uncle asked him to come live with him, which he gladly took him up on. Living with him gave him the time and the money to go to school and learn English. He was looking forward to becoming a U.S. citizen. When he finally was able to fly there, in the cabin of the plane, he said coming off you could smell freedom in the air.

After being in the States for a few months, he decided to pursue his artist's career. His uncle told him that in the '60's, which is when he was there, New Mexico was the seat of artistry. With his uncle's help, he bought a ticket to Santa Fe and off he went, seldom to return home again.

He met a Hopi there named Sits in Eagle's Claw. She made jewelry sitting on the square and sold it in Ortega's. He got a job paining murals and vases in a couple shops from there, fell in love and married her. They had four children, three boys and one girl, and led quite the artist's life. He named his oldest boy after Eduardo, hoping against hope that he wasn't dead, but especially that he wasn't under Castro's thumb.

They had both talked about the possibilities, and no matter what, getting away from Castro was what they both wanted most.

The End

Peggy Marceaux

SUPERPOWER OF A GENERATION

SUPERPOWER OF A GENERATION

In the heart of the Neolithic Period, something had spawned an unusual creature. It was an anomaly, to say the least, for when it reached maturity, it would span the length of some fifty feet and motor through the depths of the Gulf of Mexico, the Atlantic, Lake Michigan, the Pacific Ocean, and wherever, with six flipper-like appendages. Apparently, it was also seen in the Baltic Sea, the Irish Sea, Baffin Bay and the Tasmanian Sea. In '45, pretty much every body of water had a siting by young men fishing or surfing.

Fast forward to the end of WWII, to the start of the baby boom, when all the soldiers got home, and you have the ground work laid for our story. Steven "Dusty" Baker was the first born of Corp. and Mrs. Baker, coming into this world at seven pounds, nineteen and a half inches.

Dusty led a normal, uneventful life, went to Franklin School in the small coastal town of Cameron, Louisiana, from kindergarten to his middle-school years, picking up friends along the way. He played baseball and basketball, and was active in the French

81

and Debate clubs. He also had a girlfriend, named Louise. Beyond that Dusty was busy with homework and chores around the house that he shared with a brother and sisters, who were a good deal younger than he. When Dusty had time, his dad would let him go to the wharf and fish with his friends. His friends were just normal, happy go lucky boys who watched the old tube TV, like he did, that came out in the fifties their fathers buying for them, though, not without complaining that it cost some $400.

They watched common shows like I Love Lucy, Leave it to Beaver, Father Knows Best and, their favorite, Gun Smoke.

When he looked forward to graduating from high school, he knew college was out of the question because his mother made only $5,000 a year as a school teacher, and his dad made only a tad more as a mechanic where he worked on crank cars and more modern cars in the Dodge line.

Dusty was only a C student, though not much had changed in his life except the more modern TV and some of its programs. So, Dusty had taken to spending a lot more time at the dock, fishing with his friends. After all, he was bringing food in for the family. On one of those days, an "odd" thing happened.

They had just come back from buying some bait and a couple of six packs of Schlitz, of which they had already popped a few on the way back to the dock and gulped them down. From what they saw, they had begun to think that the alcohol had already gone to their heads. Dusty looked out at the water and stopped in his tracks.

"Hey, guys, what am I looking at straight ahead?" Dusty squinted his eyes. All were quiet as they looked out over the water. An eerie sensation started to creep all through them. They saw and felt a whirling sound surround the thing in the water. The water had also turned a strange shade of green and swirls had begun to ripple out away from the beast toward the edges of the water.

"Gosh, I don't know. What IS that?" Stewart asked flabbergasted.

"Wish I'da brought my camera," said Frank. "There's no way my father'll believe this."

Best way they could describe it was that "it looked like a long snake just below the surface of the water. But, its length, man, just went on and on, "I'd say some forty-five or fifty feet." Dusty had described to his dad. "And the *speed*, I'll bet it was moving at a good clip, somewhere between twenty-five and thirty miles an hour, with only those six flipper-like appendages."

His dad gave him a hard look.

Dusty turned to face him full on; "I know what you're thinking, but I kid you not," he said very seriously.

What they didn't know was this was also happening around the world. That there was a secret Operation called "51" in Nevada just north of Lake Groom, but by his time, had increased to numbers 52, 53, and 54, and then from there had gone into a massive underground network of tunnels all the way from Colorado, to Roswell, New Mexico, and then to Cheyenne, Wyoming.

And, at just that moment, while he was telling his dad what he saw, Dusty, though he had never heard of any of this before, started in on how he'd build a model 3 Tesla engine.

His dad asked, "Wait a minute, Son. What's a Tesla engine?"

Dusty shook his head. "I don't know. But I know what one looks like when you take it apart and then put it back together."

"Well, why don't you tell me about it, then maybe we can figure it out together," his dad responded.

"Okay," Dusty replied, "I can buy a cheap engine," his dad broke in with "where at?"

"I don't know, yet," Dusty answered, "anyway, you take the motor apart and get a blue coolant that drains out. Catch the coolant to replace it. Then take the super cap off and remove the yellow rod. When the cap is off, make sure the motor turns. Then slide the whole shell off to expose all the rings and gears. Then you take everything apart in sections. That allows you to see inside it. Then you crack the motor open with a giant screw driver, and you see the all grooves where the torque comes from. To put it back together reverse what you did to take it apart, keeping in mind that the blue liquid is coolant, and the red is oil.

"After that you decide on whether you want a fast Tesla, and if you do, you want to put two batteries in the back, one for each wheel. But, if speed is not what you want, one battery will suffice for the two tires in front. All of it is run on electricity."

"A car running on electricity?" his dad asked.

"That's what my mind tells me."

"You're either nuts or a damn genius," his dad told him. "But, based on your grades, I can hardly call you a genius. And, I've never heard you use the word suffice before."

"Okay, now do you want to hear the motor dimensions to building a Mercedes Benz, a Ferrari and a Bentley?" Dusty asked.

"No, thanks," his dad declined. "I've heard enough," and he took out a Lucky Strike, then struck a match to it before he took a long drag, thinking about what he just heard.

Dusty further told his dad he knew about the up and coming 21st century cell phone and washer and dryer, though he was befuddled. He was never more than a C student in school in his life. He needed a note pad and in a hurry. Later, when he met with his friends at the soda shop, he learned they were thinking the same things. *Could it be because they saw that thing yesterday? And were having the very same thoughts, just hadn't told their folks.* They wondered now.

Frank went home and sat his folks down. He was mostly a B student so Dusty thought he'd be more believable. He told his folks that "he knew of another type of phone coming in the 21st century." At first, they laughed, but when he didn't, they started to take him more seriously.

He told them "Cell phones wouldn't have to be attached to anything. That they worked off big towers that picked up waves like radio waves and converted your voice into an electrical signal, which then put it on a carrier wave. A tiny microphone in the cell you'd be holding converts voices into electrical signals, which are then turned into strings of numbers by micro-, which means small, chips inside the phone. The signals carrying voice, text, which means like typing, digital data, like pictures, are transmitted to the receiver of it all on radio waves from one device to the other."

His parents sat there with their mouths agape. His father cleared his throat, and then he asked his son if he was sure this wasn't some theory they had read about at school? Frank assured him he had never even dreamed about it until he had seen that creature in the water. It affected the boys all in the same way.

At his house, Stewart was watching his mother wash clothes. Her washer had a roller on it, and he was hoping she wouldn't catch her hand in it.

"You know, Mom, in the 21st century, they will have electric washers that will just wait to be stuffed with clothes, have the water level set, the heat set, then the delicacy set before it's turned on. Then they will have dryers that tumble while they dry clothes and will only need to be told how many minutes and how hot you want it before it's started." Stewart was a straight A student, where Dusty was just a C student.

"Oh," she said "are you doing this for a school paper?"

"No," he said, "but maybe I should, since it will come true. I've just known about it since the guys and I saw that creature in the water."

Nick, one of Dusty's fishing buddies, talked to his parents, too. "You know ever since I saw that strange creature in the water, I've been having visions. One of them is of people riding on motorized skis. You know where you sit on this thing on the water that's small, but has a motor you can't see. You can turn it on and move around in the water by yourself, and sometimes you can work up to a pretty good speed. So much so that they have competitions where you have to run up and off a ramp, or follow a course laid out for you to see who can beat everyone else out?"

Nick had his parents held in suspense as he told them about his visions since the siting.

He had passed all his Advanced Placement classes and was, therefore, worthy of being believed.

"Also, I see high rises, tall buildings, taller than anything else, where people work at the top and wealthy people own what they call penthouses, which is just another word for fancy apartments.

You have regular apartments in the buildings, too, towards the bottom. Also, shockingly, we will be attacked on September 11, 2001 in just such high rises. Osama bin Laden, a Saudi-born militant leader of al-Qaeda, designated as a terrorist group by NATO, will mastermind the attack.

He had some men learn to fly planes and then get tickets to board four of our passenger jets without incident on that day. When they did, they hijacked four of them and two of them headed straight to what was known as the twin towers, because they stood tall, at the same height, side by side; then a third one headed to the Pentagon, and a fourth headed to the Capitol, but thanks to brave men on board, they stormed the cockpit and crashed it before it could hit the Capitol.

Thanks to cell phones most people on board those planes could call their loved ones and say good bye.

"The twin towers will be hit first, which will alarm all Americans. They won't know what's going on; neither will the second President Bush. The towers, which, as you might imagine, will explode and catch fire where, either everyone would be burned alive or jump out of windows and choose a different kind of death. Then, the towers will crumble to ashes, which will make for a mass clean-up that will last for years and contribute to many future lung diseases.

As well, our President Bush will over-react by wrongly dropping bombs on Iraq to kill Saddam Hussein, who will be innocent in all this. Unfortunately, it will kill many Iraqi people, but not Hussein, whom they will find shielding himself in an underground hidey-hole."

His parents were horrified. "How can we prevent this, and who is al-Qaeda?" his father asked.

"I don't know; I just know al-Qaeda had most everything to do with it." Nick answered.

At Jack's house, the winner of the vocabulary contest at his high school was telling his parents "that someday in the future anybody will be able to buy military-style rifles; that children, mentally-ill people and whoever has a vendetta against a certain kind of people, will be able to go into their churches or elementary schools, or bars, or grocery stores, or wherever, and shoot up multiple maybe dozens of people with no provocation, except that they are Jewish, or Gay, or a strict disciplinarian."

Jack said, "It's too early, Mom. You teach us right from wrong, and we don't have access to military rifles, so you guys have done a good job. It's the parents in the future who will bear the responsibility."

Meanwhile young men in their country and other countries around the world were doing the same thing. They all knew the now of things, and when they saw the creature, they knew the what of the future, but didn't know how to get from here to there. They learned that planes could be built, but did not have the expertise to build them; the same with airports and hangars for the planes. They learned that skyscrapers could be erected, but did not know how to erect them.

They knew that food chains could be established and shopping centers could be planned, but couldn't enlist anyone younger to help them out. They also couldn't get professors to believe them. They had a lifetime's worth of knowledge to teach universities the formulas, but their students seemed oblivious to what they were teaching, or didn't care what they were telling them. They were expending their energy for nothing, because, alas, they didn't know how to pass it on.

In the interim, Dusty's dad had researched everything he could on Operation 51, 52, 53 and so on, in Nevada near Lake Groom. He broke into the network on his short-wave radio about what was underground in the tunnels. He told no one. Dusty's dad was able to break into their signals, a difficult thing to do with top secret government operations. What he intercepted made his hair curl: area 51 is called Home Airport and the overall area is called Groom Lake; "It is obviously off limits to the public," said a National Historian. He further called Groom Lake a dry salt bed, where unidentified flying objects are drawn to and crashed, and where their alien bodies were studied, but it never really explained what's really going on at site 51: He did learn that "The underground tunnel that they developed after Site 51 has a deep lake in it where scientists witness and nurture an ancient species of a prehistoric creature; they try to keep it from escaping into our water ways, but often without success."

Unbelievably, Dusty's dad decided to go to Nevada, telling his family he had to take a trip for his work. Dusty's father, who was named Mac, made his way to the forbidden gate of Operation 51. He knew he would be fined $600 if found near there and that there were armed guards securing the place.

But he was more interested in the tunnel than anything else, and managed to make his way close to and hide away from the guard behind some excavated dirt. He climbed the fence when the guard wasn't looking, went into the tunnel and down to the deep lake. It was eerie and dark. He heard some splashing about and cursed himself for not bringing a flashlight. Mac inched his way in a little farther and squinted his eyes; he took a cigarette match out and stuck it.

What he saw made the hair on his neck stand on end. It was a large snake-like creature turning in front of him with its large flippers, and eyeing him. Mac tried to back up more, but it wasn't in time, for the huge, snake creature reached out and grabbed him by its fearsome teeth, swallowing him whole.

For two days, Mac's family was desperate to find him. They called the police and all the neighbors, but had no luck. It was like he just disappeared into the sky, or dropped off the earth.

Dusty was sick. He thought it may have something to do with what he told his dad, but he couldn't imagine what. He found his dad's short-wave radio and checked it out to see if it could tell him something. His blood ran cold when he guessed what his dad had planned to do. He told some of his buddies who agreed to join him in going to Nevada, but they didn't know what they would do after they got there. Dusty did. He brought a flashlight, his .270, some shells, and bought a silencer.

They found where Operation 51 was on a map. It clearly said: "Off Limits. Highly Classified. $600 fine if found near it, and a bullet doesn't find you first." That shook some of the boys up, but not Dusty. He wanted to save his father, if he could. Like his dad, they went at night, parked away from the place, and snuck up to the fence near the first tunnel. When the guard turned away, one went over the fence and hid. When the guard turned away again, the next one went over. And, again, when he turned away for the third time, the last one was in the process of doing the same thing when his shirt got snagged.

"Halt!" hollered the guard. But Dusty came up on the guard from behind with a large stick and started to choke him. A short struggle ensued; the guard pulled, not just the stick, but Dusty to the ground. Still, Dusty never let go of the stick, nor his pressure on the guard's throat.

The guard finally dropped his rifle and then fell down himself, dead. They didn't need his rifle, since they brought their own with a silencer on it. The other two boys stood there, shaken that he'd killed a man.

"Shit!" Nick exclaimed. "I didn't sign up for this!"

Dusty said, "What are you waiting for? Let's go!"

The tunnel was dark and bleak just like it was for Mac, the difference was Dusty had a flashlight. When they got down to the deep lake, Dusty saw his dad's pack of cigarettes and, on the ground, found the spent match.

"Oh, man," said Dusty. "This is not a good sign." Dusty sat on a rock outcropping and put his face in his hands. They could see his shoulders shake. Frank went over to him and put his hand on his shoulder to comfort him. After a bit, Dusty rubbed his eyes and said: "Let's get this over with. I don't see it anywhere. There aren't even any swirls, but it's got to be in here since it just killed my dad. He must be sleeping on the bottom; let's wake him up to a surprise ambush."

And, they started throwing a barrage of rocks and stones into the water. One after another, they were unrelenting. Finally, the beast came up with its mouth open wide just as Fred had thrown a rock, biting his arm off. Fred cried out in pain. Nick quickly whipped off his belt and hurriedly put a tourniquet around the rest of his arm, then Dusty started bearing down on the creature, while Fred whimpered, who surprisingly stayed up with his mouth open as a threat to the boys. Dusty fired one .250 round directly into his mouth, slid the bolt back to eject the spent shell, slid another in and fired again, this time at his head. Dusty continued firing, reloading and then firing again. Finally, the creature went belly up and was still.

At that moment Frank and Dusty turned toward Fred and, Nick, who was sitting with him, and hurried Fred out of the tunnel. He had lost quite a bit of blood and was in shock.

They scoped the place outside of the tunnel and felt safe about taking him to the fence. Dusty and Nick developed a method to carry him over it and get him to the car. Soon as they were down town they took him to the South Cameron Memorial Hospital. From there, Dusty called his parents. He thought that was the hardest thing he'd ever have to do besides telling his mother that his dad was dead. He was wrong.

When he got home, his mother was waiting anxiously. He laid his rifle against the wall and carefully released the handful of spent shells on the table. His mother covered her mouth.

But, when he pulled his dad's Lucky Strikes out of his pocket, and laid it down by the shells, she broke out crying hysterically. Dusty sat her in a nearby chair, and knelt down to put his head into her lap and cry with her.

As the days went by, it was taking Fred longer to get over the loss of his arm than the doctors thought it would. Sure, he would grieve the missing body part, and even have phantom pain, but there was something else at play here. He started to have strange burn marks across that shoulder and his chest. The marks blistered up and acted peculiar, like he had been in a fire. In fact, they burned him he had been in a fire. Had the boys just driven to the front of the Site, they would have seen the hazardous sign that warned of radiation. But, the boys didn't and had no idea what those marks were from. Neither had the doctors, who just treated it like a burn, not knowing that the radiation was eating the boy from the inside out.

Dusty and Frank were just glad they hadn't been found out – yet – and were happy to get back to fishing, though the murder hung over Dusty's head ever since that night. It was a welcome relief after Mr. Baker's Memorial Service to go down to the wharf again. Things had been heavy around there for so long, a fishing line seemed like an old friend had come back into town. They couldn't bring themselves to enjoy another beer, though. It just wasn't right with

Fred suffering so. All they could do was say the next fish was for Fred, until a fish came floating up near the dock.

"What's the matter with that fish?" asked Frank.

It was obvious the fish was dying. They looked closely; it looked like it was scalded.

"Oh, my God, Frank, I think it's dying from radiation poisoning."

"Aren't you just jumping the gun a bit?"

"Then you look closely at it?"

They both took their poles out of the water, and threw the fish they had caught back in.

"Man, I've been poisoning my family with those fish this whole time," said Frank, despondent.

"You aren't alone," Dusty told him.

Before the month was out, Nick had something suspicious show up on his hands. He had been closest to Fred after the creature had bitten off his arm, though they didn't think of that then. He had blisters show up on his palms in little circles. They began to burn him something awful. Nick went to the doctor who seemed baffled. In his mind, Nick had stuck his hand in a fire. Nick assured him he did no such thing, so the doctor had him admit to everywhere he'd been in the last two months. Of course, Nick couldn't do that to Dusty, so he left the doctor dumbfounded. However, that was before the fish started washing up onto shore.

"Well, they are burns, Son, that's for sure. We'll just have to treat them like burns."

As time went on, Nick's burns spread over this body as Fred's had done, and gone deeper into his cells. A doctor at the hospital finally put his finger on Fred being burned by radiation. That scared all the boys who were there plenty. Finally, Nick had to tell his doctor where they'd gone and that told him where the radiation had come from. In the hospital, Fred was terribly ill. In fact, they didn't give him long to live. Nick was really scared the same thing would happen to him. So, he'd called Dusty's house and asked to speak to Dusty, after he had offered his condolences to Mrs. Baker, again. While he waited, he posted a sign up on the dock that said: **Don't eat the seafood: radiation poison**.

"Nick," he said. "We need to talk. No. In person. I'll wait for you at the dock. Yes, today. I'd say it is very important, so drop what you're doing."

When Dusty arrived, he asked, "What's so important?"

Nick showed Dusty his hands, his chest and the other side of his face. Dusty's eyes grew wide.

"Yeah, and who's to say you won't be next," predicted Nick.

"Oh, man, did you tell the doctor where that came from?" asked Dusty, horrified.

"I had to, man. They aren't just burns like they treated Fred for all these months. I don't want to die. I had to tell him the truth."

"How much of the truth did you tell him?" asked Dusty, guarded.

"Only that we had gone poking around at Operation 51. He said that was a radiation hazardous site. I didn't know that, did you? That's all he knows," replied Nick.

"No, I didn't know that. Oh, man. The creature is dead, but is exacting its vengeance on us still."

"I just hope it doesn't wipe us all out," Nick said, scared and shaking.

"Maybe the doc has caught yours in time," Dusty said, sounding hopeful.

"I can always keep my fingers crossed, while I still have them. Look, I only got an hour's reprieve away from the hospital. I have to go back now. Thanks for coming."

Dusty felt so guilt-ridden he almost wanted to turn himself in, but he just couldn't do that to his mother. By the time Nick returned to the hospital, Fred had died. That was a huge blow to all of them. Nick got out an hour to attend the funeral. That's all. Frank and Dusty were always examining themselves in their bathrooms. Their parents were asking themselves why it was taking the boys longer than usual for them to clean up?

Dusty had been in to see Nick a couple of times since he was admitted to South Memorial. It was a terribly awful thing to see two of your buddies who had simply agreed to accompany you to the tunnels get fried before your eyes. Nick's illness followed the same course as Fred's, so naturally everyone expected it to end in the same way. That put even more guilt on Dusty. On his last visit he told Nick he was so sorry, and that he loved him before he walked out of his room. He walked out of the hospital, stepped over on the grass and threw up. It took only another week before the radiation killed him. The funeral was almost too much for Dusty to take.

He seriously considered not going to it, but that would be a slap in the face to a dead man, whom he loved very much.

Soon, Frank started exhibiting radiation signs. His appeared first on his face, then moved on to his chest. Frank was horrified. He'd done nothing but go into the tunnel; there was no contact with Fred or Nick. His parents were stunned and befuddled.

"Why?" They asked.

"I guess because we were in a radiation zone. We were warned, but failed to see the sign," he admitted.

"Oh, Frank," his mother had sobbed.

"It's okay, Mom, I'll beat this." But he didn't beat it. As the days went by, his radiation burns spread, too.

Dusty was preparing his mom for the worse. He didn't know when it would happen to him, but he was sure it would.

Weeks went by when he'd visit his friend, Frank, in the hospital. All he could say was

"I'm so sorry, man."

Frank wanted to know if they were still fishing at the dock.

"No, Frank, nobody can do that anymore. And, you and your folks don't try to eat "em either."

Within a month, Frank had died. Yet, another funeral Dusty and his friends had to attend. Dusty was waiting, almost willing his turn to come around. *Better than living with all this guilt*, he thought. The weight of it had made him into a sullen, irritable human being.

But, the more he examined himself, the less he found. In fact, it was like every blemish he had ever had had cleared up. "No!" he cried out loud to no one in the bathroom.

He came out and threw himself into a soft chair in the living area.

"Gosh, Dusty, I wish I knew what is making you so miserable," his mother had said.

Lost in his own thoughts, he didn't even acknowledge she was there, much less that she had said something to him. He just let himself go, he grew a beard, which got bushier by the day; he wouldn't eat, he couldn't sleep, he wouldn't stay clean. Then there was Frank's funeral to attend, for which he looked horrible. Everyone commented on it to those standing closest to them.

The last time he saw himself in the mirror, he grew so angry that he reared back with his fist and hit it so hard it broke. His mother had to doctor his hand because he wouldn't go to the doctor himself. Not one, he thought. Not one mark of radiation, and I deserve it, not all my friends who were only there to support me.

Months went by, and Dusty did not get the radiation "curse." Nor did the police ever discover who strangled the guard. Dusty's mom eventually died, which was yet another funeral to attend. His brother and sisters wanted nothing to do with him, so he ended up on the streets.

Had Dusty not been so caught up in his on misery, he would have realized that Jack and Stewart had also succumbed to radiation poisoning.

Dusty was shrinking up from not eating and drinking. His friends and his family blamed him for their deaths. When 2045 rolled around, and made him

100 years old, he still carried all that guilt around like it was fresh guilt, still weighing heavily on his shoulders. Then, 2145 came and went making him, 200 years old, still without sleep or food. He was basically mummified by then. When 2245 came around, and he was 300 years old, knowing he still couldn't sleep or eat, he also knew it was the creature plaguing him with the deaths of everybody in his home town, forever. And, for him, forever seemed to be literarily that. How else could he explain it? *And, what kind of progress was that? One generation's worth of knowledge and energy, received and blown away by a curse from a supernatural source?* thought Dusty. *Better to have the* what *and the* when *come with the* how *as time sorts it all out; yes, rather than pursuing a curse, better to let time run its course.* He never realized that he and his father had changed the course of history by killing the creature, the same creature that had killed many young men of his generation who had seen it around the world.

The End

It was a Stark and Corny Night

It was a Stark and Corny Night

The murder went down at a speakeasy in the Suburbs of New York. A sleek, leggy woman was talking to a gumshoe about the perpetrator He made sure the victim was black, and LGBTQ member, Muslim, a Christian a Jew, a musician, or a cop. Those were the parameters of the hate groups, there were so many heavily armed hate groups running wile, it was hard to keep up with them all. After his cup of corning Joe, he grabbed his hat, raked his hand through his hair again and drive it five plus miles into the ruins of old New York where the woman lived.

He passed Opies on the streets, sleeping in their cardboard beds or stoned and openly having sex. They were groups of homeless people living off the government. The Chanks were hate groups easily distinguishable by the Uncle Sam vests that had a picture of him in his red shirt and blue vest saying I Want to Get You. Chanks were hard to arrest since they'd rather commit suicide to further their causes than be caught. Anyway, they didn't waste their strychnine, heroin or cocaine on the pies; just let the elements and street drugs take care of them they thought.

When he reached the bottom of the elevator, Cobb rang the intercom, "Detective Ty Cobb here to talk with you about the speak easy murder," he said into the intercom.

"503," she answered in a sexy voice.

The elevator was filled with cigarette fumes, and that didn't bode well for him. Thats when a shot rang out. This one was so loud and near that the bullet broke he her window upstairs and grazed the lady's arm.

"Ahhh!" she gasped.

He just ran through her door uninvited. Cigarette fumes spilled from the room, opened the window (cough) and checked down the nine floors on the street below; then, he hurriedly ran to the door and opened it wide. Nothing. (cough) Afterwards, he closely examined the wall behind her and dug out the corn kernel with his pocket knife.

"Hmm," he said to himself. (cough). "A .38 caliber; must have been fired from a Saturday Night Special." Finally, he attended to her arm. "Why is this person (cough) after you?"

She took another long drag from her opera cigarette holder. (cough) (cough)

The raspy voice started up again. This time it was terrified. More personal "Yes. He had on a fedora pulled down over his eyes, but I could still see a perfectly manicured moustache and goatee under it. He wore a gray, double breasted suit, with spats over his shoes.'

"Well, you could see that from way up here> That's going to be hard to differentiate him from most men. (cough) Maybe the goatee will single him out."

"Oh, I forgot. He had a scar on his right cheek. Kind of like he had been cut by a knife some time ago."

"Okay. There's something else to go on. And I think I had just asked you about his height when the shot interrupted us."

She answered him in obvious pain. "Around five feet five to seven; I'm really not sure."

"Okay, and (cough) thank you. I feel like I've taken too much of your time already. You really ought to have a doctor come over here and take (cough) a better look at that arm. I'm sorry about your window,"

"A window is fixable, even though I'm on the tenth floor," she muttered. "By the way you should see a doctor about that cough."

"You know, I don't think I caught your name, "he inquired.

"Crurophilia Gams," she replied (cough) "I hope I can count on you as a witness in a court of law," he told her.

"Of course," she said, and blew smoke into his face.

He tipped his hat as a 'goodbye for now' and saw himself out. Next stop was the coroner to compare the kernels and confirm the cause of death. *So glad to be out of that smoke. Woman will be dead at 35. Crurophilia, what an odd name.*

He arrived at the hospital, entered and turned left, directly to the coroners. The detective removed his hat and introduced himself. "Hello, Dr Barlow.

"I'm Detective Cobb. I've been assigned to this case. Nasty one, isn't it?"

"Oh, detective, you don't know the half of it," he replied.

"How so?" And, Detective Cobb walked over to the corpse lying face up on the gurney.

"Well, for one thing the kernel was shot into his ear, where it rattled n there and while, went to his brain and did a number in there, ended up in one nostril, traveled to the other, then to his heart."

"How could it have ended up in his heart?" asked the detective?

"I don't know. Corn kernels can do strange things; That's why more criminals are going to then. They are more lethal than bullets because of their unpredictability."

"Hmm," said Cobb. "This will be a real challenge. It's my first case with corn. Well, can I at least compare the kernel.

"You have one to compare it to?" the doctor remarked, looking surprised.

"Yes. I dug it out of the wall at a witness' home who was shot at while was there."

"I wish I'da known that before I gave it to my dog," and he hung his head.

The detective rolled his eyes.

"Well." said the coroner, "It looked like any other raw, corn kernel." The doctor defended himself.

"Tell that to the jury when I'm presenting my .38 caliber kernel." Detective Cobb came back.

"That's another reason criminals are switching to them; you can't measure them by caliber."

Every bit of the blood drained from Detective Cobb's face, "Wow," he said. "What do you have to do? Catch them in the act."

"Sure, looks like it," the coroner agreed.

"Guess I'll have to step up surveillance," he told the doc before he left.

When he got back to the police station, he enlisted the help of his half-canine, half- human, whom he name StepandFetcit, to help him learn where the corn was coming from and how they used it to kill. After a number of trips to feed stores, StepandFetchit came back to report that all the corn kernels had come from the Horse's Tail Organization, a syndicated company in ca-hoots with criminal activity and big money.

To prove that and to change that, they had to show, beyond a shadow of doubt, that the kernels had calibers and associate the kernels to that organization. Cobb asked his AI (Artificial Intelligence) about it and it sided with the doctor. Still Cobb thought only gun powder could, like a bullet, make a corn kernel move at that speed. they started looking for gunpowder that would project a .38 and .45, and started checking that the hammers and the pins were relating properly for firing the guns. they were guessing at how much powder would be needed to fire a .38. if it did more damage; it would be considered a .44 or higher. that would go a long way into measuring what had been shot. at that time, the leggy woman with the Lauren Becall voice entered the station, swinging her hips and blowing out a stream of smoke.

Cobb couldn't stand it. He needed air.

"Well, hello Ms. Gams. StepandFetchit and I were just going outside to test these two corn kernels," Cobb told her.

"May I join you. I'm all alone at home and I'm just bored to tears without men in my life."

"Sure," he told her. "What we are doing won't be very entertaining but you're welcome to come, Gams."

"Please call me by my first name," she asked him.

"Alright, Crurophilia," Cobb said and hoped he hadn't butchered it.

She pulled her silvery blonde hair back and said, "Bring it on," then she took another long drag of her cigarette, aimed it at the heavens and blew it out long and slow.

For the first time, that gave Cobb chills. "You do know you're taking your life in your hands being out like this?"

"I want to be here, especially when my lives at stake."

He looked at her and felt an immediate attraction. Her jeans were tight on that particular day, which made her legs go on forever. Her blouse was short, which gave him a peek at her navel.

I think she's flirting with me, he thought.

"Oh, I know. You made that perfectly clear." She assured him.

"Okay. Just wanted to remind you *about whatever it was I said."* He was so befuddled he had forgotten what he told her.

Cobb turned to shoot off his first round and to compare it to the round he dug out of Gam's wall.

The two kernels had a minimal amount of damage caused by a shot. Then he shot off a kernel with more gun powder. That kernel had much more damage.

"Whamo!" cried Cobb. "Kernels have calibers after all; if not a true caliber, at least more damage to it than the other. StepandFetchit, this calls for a beer!"

StepandFetchit had been thirsty for one all day, so he went ahead to their usual speak easy ahead of them.

After putting his guns away to be cleaned at a later time, Cobb and Gam started walking slowly in the direction of the old speak easy, just making small talk. In the interim StepandFetchit caught up with them, His tongue was hanging out of his mouth, and he was panting, "I've just come from (pant) the speak easy, someone was in there was firing up the place with an old (pant) AK-47. The thing is (pant) he had adjusted the long gun to fire whole corn cobs (pant). He was mowing people down with it (pant). He put his hand on his knees. "I escaped by the 'hair of my chinny chin chin' (pant)."

Cobb just stood there staring. "An old AK-47? Adapted to spraying one whole corn cob at a time?"

StepandFetchit stood. "Yes, Sir."

"I need to run over there with StepandFetchit. You need to stay away from there. In fact, go home, for now," and Cobb ran to the speakeasy. StepandFetchit followed after running to the station to get guns.

"Oh, this is getting exciting!" Gams exclaimed with glee.

After seeing the result of the onslaught and taking down evidence, Cobb went home and spent the night working with his AI on his false premise. He received nothing. So, he left the AI on all night and went to bed until well into the morning. When he awoke, he had his robotic make him coffee, strong and black. He felt awful, like a truck hit him. When he checked his communication board, he froze mid sip. Five calls were from Crurophilia, which didn't surprise him, but the one that concerned him was from his boss. *Oh shit. That was fifteen minutes ago.*

Need to call him now. He quickly punched in 1964512.

"Agent CKS 772.37. Yes, Sir. So sorry, Sir. I came home after midnight very tired, Sir."

"I checked your cell, too. I think your AI told me you were asleep. So, I hear we had a problem with an old speak easy near you?" asked his boss.

"Yes, Sir. The Chanks used whole cobs to mow down a crowd with an old AK-47."

"Can we get a handle on this, Ty?" further asked his boss.

"Oh, yes, Sir. I've got my AI on it. I pretty much wasted some time yesterday chasing the premise that, like bullets, kernels have a caliber and are projected by gun powder. I think I'm going to have to change that premise, it would help to have that weapon in my hands, though.

It's a rather antiquated AK-47. I'll have to see where my AI tells me to get one, and then to tell me how it managed to shoot off a whole cob laced with strychnine."

"Good luck. Let me know if there's anything I need to know on my end." and he signed off.

When Cobb disengaged, he glanced at his AI, then took a double take. It hit him right between the eyes.

"Oh, good grief," he said aloud.

He punched in StepandFetchit's number. "You've got to come over here and see this," he said and disengaged from the call.

Before Cobb left the board he called Gams. She berated him for five minutes for not calling he back.

"Alright, alright, I'm calling you now, so hello. No, you weren't the first I called. I had to call my boss first. He called me fifteen minutes ago, and I was late calling him. Yes, it was very important. No, let's meet at the station. I have some business there. Okay, Crurophilia. Yes, see you soon."

When he disengaged from her call, StepandFetchit was knocking at his door. Cobb opened it for him to step in.

"Take a look at my AI, will you," Cobb told his assistant.

"Oh my gosh, what a simple solution," StepandFetchit said.

"I know it. I've been kicking myself since I've seen this. Any carnival kid could have thought this one up. We've been way overthinking this, Step. Go and get me a drug—starved Opie so I can buy a couple of those Ak-47s on the black market. And, the kid's got to be bright enough to be up-to-date on with special weapons. Make sure the kid wants drugs badly, too. I'll look up the contact, and tell him I'll give him half the money now and half when he brings the weapons to me. You know the amount we promise those Opies." Then he told his assistant where to drop the Opie off.

"You've got it," said StepandFetchit, who turned to leave.

"Oh, and, Step, bring the boy down to the police station. I don't want to involve my home in any way," remarked Cobb.

"Understood," then StepandFetchit walked out the door and closed it behind him. Cobb was trying to put the pieces in place for what he'd have to do next. Who was in the network for the black market? The corn kernels were new, and the whole cob newer. And, he'd have to find someone not in the system to find that kind of antiquated long gun, but who? He met half the challenge already; he'd worry about the other half with his AI.

He found a black-market contact; he was ready for Step to bring the boy. He was raking his hand through his hair again when Crurophilia came in. *'Cleanliness was next to Godliness,' and oral hygiene were strong points, but they'd have to become stronger points if he ever wanted to kiss Crurophilia any time soon. He never thought he'd be attracted to a smoker, but, actually, that was the only part of her that galled him. Maybe he could talk her out of it.'*

"Hello, Crurophilia, you're looking sharp," Cobb told her.

She was wearing jeans so tight he didn't know how she got into them. And, this time more than her navel was visible. He looked up a little ways and spotted cleavage. He would have been embarrassed for her if he didn't like it so much. She was still sporting that opera cigarette holder, and taking long, slow drags of it before releasing the smoke toward the ceiling. *Glad I have a nice, tall ceiling in here,* Cobb thought, gratefully. She turned towards him, put her arms around his neck and gave him a slow lick and kiss on his lips. He thought his knees would buckle.

"I'm really glad to see you," she said in that raspy voice.

"I'm really glad to see you, too, Crurophilia," replied Cobb. "And don't get me wrong, I loved that, but I have a serious problem her at work that I have to attend to first before I can play."

The smoke started filtering down.

"Oh rats," she said. "I was afraid you'd say that. It would have been better to meet at your apartment I think."

"Yes, for kissing, no (cough) my work. I've got to (cough) find someone who will sell me (cough) a special gun that shoot corn cobs," lamented Cobbs.

"You mean kernels?" she asked.

"No, (cough) I mean cobs. At the speak easy they shot off at whole cob at once (cough), and my AI told me something a fourth grader would (cough) have known," and Cobb rolled his eyes.

"Oh, don't be so hard on yourself." She cupped his face. "By the way, did you not see a doctor about that cough, yet?"

"We've got to talk (cough) about that," he told her.

Just at that moment, StepandFetchit pulled up. "But it will have to wait (cough). "Cobb told Gams.

StepandFetchit walked in. "I've got one."

"A bright one?" asked Cobb.

"He outshone the moon," StepandFetchit replied.

"Okay," Cobb replied. "Bring him (cough) in here."

StepandFetcht called the boy in, and Cobb gave him the contact, then. reiterated that these weapons have to shoot off whole cobs, not just individual kernels. The teen laughed; Cobb grabbed him by his dirty tee shirt and pulled him up into his face and said something derogatory to him. The young man was set back on his feet and given $1K. Cobb had a band made of metal clipped to his ankle to be removed when he returns with the weapons.

"Thank you, Step. Now I'm going back to my apartment (cough) so my AI can teach me how to load whole cobs."

After telling StepandFetchit where to drop the boy off, Cobb and Crurophilia walked to their respective cars holding hands.

Once at the apartment, Crurophilia said, "I remember you saying we need to talk," and she took another drag of her cigarette.

"Crurophilia, the only thing wrong with my lungs is smoke. I just can't seem to tolerate it. When you leave, I don't cough at all. Now, I'm not saying I don't want to see you anymore, because I do. What I am saying, though is we are going to have to work out when we can be together if you keep smoking. You may have to choose if the habit is so engrained in you since you since you've been smoking so long. I'm not coughing now because my apartment is virtually smoke free, and I have a filter to keep it that way."

Crurophilia looked like someone had just told her she had stabbed them in the heart.

"Oh, my. I hadn't thought." She was just about to put the cigarette to her lips, habitually, when what he said really registered with her. Big old tears welled up in her green eyes.

"Crurophilia, I know how much you like to smoke, so I'm not asking you to give it up."

She put her cigarette out outside, came in and put her head down. Then she looked up into his soft, light-brown eyes. "But I really like you, Ty," she said. "When I'm not with you, I'm thinking about you, wondering what you're doing and longing to be with you."

"Then we have a dilemma, because, when my work doesn't distract me, I do the very same thing." He walked over to her and put an arm around her shoulders. "I won't ask you to stop smoking. That's a personal choice and rather too controlling of me. I don't have to tell you it's bad for your health, because you're a big girl, but you've been doing it a long time and that will only shorten the amount of time I'll get to spend with you."

She turned towards him and put her arms around his neck, then buried her face into his shoulder. "I'll try to break myself of the habit. It won't be pretty, so forgive me if I stay away for a while."

"Do what you need to do, Crurophilia. And, if it doesn't work, then, it doesn't work, I'll honestly be surprised if it does because you been smoking for so long. I'll take you anyway I can, though.

We may just have to spend a lot of our time outside," and he winked at her. "Now, I hate to bring this up, but I've got to check with my AI about how to load the corn cobs in these weapons I'm buying."

She asked, "Can I come watch? No cigarettes for now."

"Sure, you can," he answered.

He went to his computer and turned it on, Both Crurphilia and Ty were staring at the screen. Cobb asked his AI to give him specific instructions about where to insert the cob and how the weapon would then operate. It told him that individual kernels would be pulled off rapidly and shot out with compressed air. In addition, it said that the people staring at the screen were two biological males. Crurophilia was horrified.

"What's the matter, Crurophilia?" Cobb asked h

"What your AI said about me," she trembled. "Can all AI's say that a person is a biological male or female?"

"Yes, as of five or so years it can."

"And you're not repelled knowing that?" she further asked, timidly.

"Nope. It's not like I'm wanting to bring children up in this hideous world of ours, That's the last thing I'd want to do,"

She threw her arm around his neck, "Oh, I love you, Ty Cobb," and she kissed him hard on the mouth.

When she let him come up for air, he said, "I love you, too, Crurophilia Gams."

Later that night, StepandFetchit called asking him to come get what he ordered from the black market and to deliver the rest of the money to the Opie. He seemed very pleased. He had bought a few cobs of corn the next day from a market place, had shucked them and cleaned them good for the gun and was ready to follow the AI's instructions. Believe it or not, the job was relatively easy. *Yep,* he thought, *he was way overthinking this.*

A good two weeks went by before he heard from Crurophilia. *What if she doesn't think I'm worth the trouble?* The question had crossed his mind more than once since their last meeting.

Finally, his engagement board lit up. "Oh, hello, Crurophilia. How've you been?"

"This has been by far the hardest thing I've ever tried to do in my life. And, at that, I've fallen off the wagon a time or two," she told him.

"Just a time or two," he chuckled.

"It's NOT funny!"

"No, I know it's not. I'm sorry I laughed," he tried to sound serious.

"If you weren't worth it, I'd throw this whole thing out the window."

"Well, you still can. We haven't put a time frame around it. Heck, I'd never do that to you,"

Cobb told her.

"I know it. Besides I'm in a foul mood today. I just wanted to hear your voice."

"Thank you for letting me hear yours."

"I appreciate it. Goodbye, Ty,"

"Goodbye, Crurophilia. (a short pause) I love you." But she had already disengaged.

He sat there and stared out the window at the wall of the apartment next door. Somehow, he couldn't help but feel lonesome. The call made him sad. as though his whole life wasn't sad and unfulfilled. He stood and grabbed hold of the AK-47, loaded it with a corn cob, and albeit, the kernels were benign, pressed the air compressor on the weapon and rattled off the kernels in a barrage of explosions all around the room. He felt much better afterwards, though his room was in tatters.

No one was interested enough in him to knock on the door and check on hm. That was just as well. He was in no mood for company. He had a terrible headache, and attributed that to not eating anything, so he called in a one topping pizza. He opened a can of Guinness to go with the usual fast delivery. He took another look at his room and got sick to his stomach. He knew he alone would have to clean it up. His robotic didn't know where everything belonged. He finished his first Guinness by the time the pizza arrived, so he opened him another can. By that time his head was splitting. So, he placed the pizza on the counter, after he brushed the junk on the floor, and stood his Guinness on the stand by his bed. He took some Valzalore for his headache and fell into bed. *Oh, Crurophilia,* he thought, *why aren't you here?* as he drifted off to sleep.

The next morning, he awoke and sat straight up in bed. He had had a bad dream, mostly because it could have come true long before now. Let's say that the Chanks had been scoping Crurophilia out for a couple months now; he didn't know that, he was just sure it could be true. Hell, maybe even for longer. And, let's say Crurophilia had been confiding in a friend, let's call her Patsy, she and Ty. He didn't know those things were true, but they could have been true for a while now. Perhaps they found out Crurophilia was trans. I mean, his AI said there was a 90% level of confidence it was true, which would leave only a 4-8% margin of error; so, if she looked at anyone else's AI, it would have given her away, too. The point is, say the friend, Patsy frequented lesbian bars. There would be two strychnine, laced corn kernels waiting for them. *I mean, I'm sure Crurophilia wouldn't attend the bars because they would be smoke-filled*, he thought. She may decide to fall off the wagon one night, though. I wouldn't blame her. But what if the Chanks beat me to her apartment with a corn cob and an AK-47? Who will be there to stop them?

Cobb jumped out of bed and zipped up his jeans. Cobb couldn't wait for the black market so he asked his AI where he could get the strychnine recipe and found the bottles in, of all places, the feed store. When he got home, he quickly put on the gloves and mask and brushed it on the cobs. He made sure to throw the brush away in hazardous waste—wouldn't want an animal to get into it. Then, he headed to Crurophilia's. After parking his car, and got to the elevator all was quiet. "Oh, man, I let myself get carried away by that dream," he said out loud.

Well, she'll never forgive me if I've come by and didn't go up to see her, he thought.

So, Cobb got into the elevator, punched the tenth floor and met two Chanks coming down. Cobb brought his gun with him, but the Chanks looked like they were only on reconnaissance. When he arrived at Crurophilia's door, the softly rapped on it. After he heard some equally soft shuffling, he saw her open the door. She threw herself into his arms.

"You okay, Crurophilia? he asked.

"I am now," she whispered in his ear, sending chills down his spine.

"I mean have you had anyone bothering you?"

"Not that I know of, why?"

"Because I ran into a couple of Chanks in the elevator who looked like they were only doing some reconnaissance. Which isn't good, because they may know that you're trans. And, if you are confiding in anyone about us, well they'll be watching her, too."

Crurophilia dropped her arms and turned to go back inside. "There is one friend I've spoken to about us, but she is innocent in all this."

"Crurophilia, we're all innocent in this. Chanks don't care about justice. It's not that kind of gang," he reminded her.

"That scare me for you," she said.

"Me? What do you think it does me for you? Look. I had a bad dream about its last night. I saw clearly what could be taking place here, and, with those thugs coming down the elevator, I'm even surer about my dream now; so, tell me what time you talk to her, and I'll see if I can catch those goons listening in to your conversations, however they do it."

"I engage her about this time of day," Crurophilia answered him, scared now.

"Okay. Then, now it'll be. Oh, by the way, it sure is nice not to be coughing to death in here for a change," he said with a wry smile.

"Oh, get out of here," she said, teasingly, smiled and kicked him in the rear.

"You really need to work on that. Didn't hurt me a bit," he laughed back at her.

Several weeks went by and Cobb still hadn't heard from Crurophilia. That really bothered him. Two weeks, yes, he understood that, but several? He'd been checking on things, listening in with no luck. That bothered him, too. What had changed? More questions than answers. He'd have to make another trip out there, but he hated to do that. Still, she wasn't leaving him any choice. He drove the high rise. Again, things looked normal. He walked to the elevator, but didn't meet either Chanks or fumes. Now, things didn't seem so normal. When he arrived on her floor, he walked to her room, knocked on her door and removed his hat.

To his surprise someone else answered. He became immediately distraught.

"This used to be Crurophilia Gams' room. Do you know where she'd be?"

"No, I don't," replied an elderly lady. "Is she the one who stained this room and all the drapery with smoke?"

"I'm afraid so, but I desperately need to find her. Are you sure you don't know where she's gone?"

"I'm sure. but you can try asking the hotel manager. He's in room 107 on the first floor."

"Thank you so much," Cobb donned his hat and took the stairs to the manager's room.

He knocked on the door. When the older man answered it, Cobb flashed his badge. "Could you tell me where the woman who was living in apartment 503 has moved to?"

"Ms. Gams?"

"Yes, that's her."

"She told me she was in fear of her life and moved in with a friend."

"Can you remember her friend's name, engagement number or address?" Cobb asked.

"I don't think I have any of that."

"Well, if you ever hear from her again, please tell her to get in touch with Detective Cobb. She knows how to reach me."

Cobb spent the rest of the night drinking. He couldn't concentrate on anything or believe she would do this to him. *Maybe I could get the girl's name at a lesbian bar. I've got to something or I'll go crazy.* He picked the lesbian bar nearest him and waited until it was late.

That's when he was told the regular clientele would arrive. He drove the six or so miles to Kindred Spirits and parked his Honda as near to the door as he could, hoping it'll be seen. He cozied up to the smokie bar and ordered a Guinness. Then he just sipped with a handkerchief over his face and watched the door. An hour went by, then two. He was just about to call it a night, when the door opened and in walked a very effeminate lady with Crurophilia. *She obviously didn't see or recognize my car,* he thought. Crurophilia either was asked to or volunteered to get the drinks, at the bar. Cobb swiveled his stool around to face her as she approached. She was smoking a cigarette. She froze when she saw him, then lowered her head and came up to him.

"I couldn't do it," she said.

"Could do what? Give me a call?" he asked.

"No, I couldn't give up cigarettes."

"I thought we had a plan for that," he replied. "Or maybe, you just don't love me enough?

Maybe you love your friend more," he suggested.

"No, it's not like that," she answered.

"So, what's it like? And why do I have to learn this way?"

"I'm sorry, Ty, I really am."

131

"So. are we over? I'm still not sure."

About that time, the door swung open, and three or four Chanks came in with AK-47's, locked and loaded. Cobb instinctively scooped up Crurophilia in his arms but was mowed down right was mowed down right where he stood, holding Crurophilia. Everyone else in the bar was also battered by the poisonous corn kernels. No one escaped; not one survived. As he convulsed, Ty sought out Crurophilia's lips one last time, and she acquiesced.

The End

Charlotte's

Legacy

Charlotte's Legacy

If a god walked off a Romance novel, would you know it? You might guess he was Norse because of his shoulder-length blond hair, bright blue eyes and his coloring, but his soft features and leanness would attest to his Italian heritage, minus the Roman nose, of course. His name would be Victor Lance Vescovo, who *eventually became a self-made wealthy man by owning and investing in a private equity company.*

When Dallas-born Victor Vescovo retired in 2023 as a Commander from the Navy, he began his deep-water expeditions, along with his fiancée, Heather West, a biologist and geologist, who would join Hope Sykes in operating the Sonar Mapping Room. There Victor would see a diagram of the ocean floors, and its trenches, along with their different depths. The trenches were far deeper, like a crevasse in the ice. The sides were close, together letting something small in them only, such as Victor's miniature sub.

As an Oxford grad Heather, a stunning mulatto, was not a bit like Victor from Stanford, but maybe that was a good thing. In fact, she became an equal partner to him and got along well, as long as they were left to their own duties. The only time Heather would stick her nose in Victor's affairs was when the danger was too much for her to bear, which was often. It got so the crew of Victor's Proto Type small sub started to keep the dangers a secret from her.

After visiting the Sonar Mapping Room, where Heather and Hope had finished an echo of the ocean floor, both Victor and Patrick, the sub's builder, located the deepest part of the Atlantic Ocean. They planned to go together to investigate the Puerto Rico Trench, also known as the Brownson Deep, where the north American plate slid tectonically atop the lesser Antilles plate. Heather was glad they were going together. Patrick was the best mechanic on board, so she knew he could handle anything that came up; after all he built the sub.

The sub was the smallest made on earth, and was almost beyond destruction. It had a Russian-made titanium core protecting the crew from both freezing temperatures and all the pressure that it would have to sustain at extreme depths, yet windows to watch fauna they'd never seen before. The weather was fine on the first day, so it was an easy drop from the surface for Victor and Patrick. But, almost immediately Patrick started wiping a leak at the hatch door. The further down they dropped the harder the leak shot out water. They radioed back to the crew that they had to come back up to fix the leak. That left Victor frustrated. He just put his forehead down on the railing of the larger ship. They had already launched the device that always preceded them with bait, with a fish attached to it. It was descending down to the depth they were hoping to achieve. He was wondering what new fauna he was missing, and if it would come back for him to see.

After Patrick and the crew tightened some screws, he and Victor anxiously squeezed back through the hatch, one at a time, and shut the door. This time, the hatch held, and they were on their way down again, nice and dry. Inwardly, Victor was glad for the company. He had gotten over the claustrophobia he felt a long time ago, but he would wake at night when he felt water come into the sub, trapping. him. Though frantic, he dared not wake Heather and tell her. How could a grown man that had conquered Everest be so cowardly about a dream? Now he had someone with whom to talk, with whom to trouble-shoot, and now with whom to share exploring the new fauna. Within hours they were at the bottom of the Puerto Rico Trench, some 27,360 feet deep. Silt rose up around them, but settled pretty quickly. Victor was as excited as he was when he climbed the seven summits. What would they see at this depth? The sub slipped from the sunshine, through the twilight zone, then the midnight zone, the abysmal zine, and, finally, to the Hadal zone, equipped with lights, they watched intently. Within minutes, something slid by his window. It looked most like a form of jellyfish, kind of translucent. Then another came by. All of a sudden, a couple of flat worm fish swam up to the bait but didn't taste it. A shark, the likes of which they'd never seen, came by to investigate the bait, but the flat worms who been there first had sprayed the bait with a slime that the sharks dared not touch. The shark had no eyes, but it didn't need any within this darkest and deepest zone of the trench. Victor and Patrick thought they saw something else. They wondered what it was. Then they looked out the left window and saw it again. He put his head down as did Patrick. Victor let out a low oath. Patrick said.

"How in the hell does plastic trash get this far down?"

Victor was sick to his stomach. He grabbed the radio and told the ship's crew they were coming up.

"Then you'd better hurry. There's a storm brewing."

In the few hours it took them to come up; the water had developed a good chop. The sub bobbed around like a cork. The men had to hurry out of the sub to beat the storm, but also because the ship's crew had to attach it with a large hook on a long chain called a closing cleat, to haul it in; they couldn't do that with the hatch open. The rest of the crew was watching from the ship, including Heather and Hope. The sub kept bobbing around making it very difficult for the ICB-1, rubber-raft to latch on the tiny sub. Heather watched stoically until Victor slipped and fell into the Atlantic. She covered her mouth with her hand as if to force down a cry. The men in the ICB-1 rubber rescue boat grabbed Victor before the choppy waves could carry him far, but he was drenched and shivering.

At the restaurant in the evening, back on shore, Heather and Victor were talking about the new fauna he had seen. The waiter brought him a glass of ice water. It reminded him of the piece of trash he'd seen in the trench.

"I never went us to drink from a plastic bottle again."

"Alright," she'd said, not knowing from where that came.

He told her from where it came.

"Oh. Now I see. I don't blame you. Let's see what the Southern Trench offers up. Hopefully that'll be the last disappointment you'll have to endure," and she put her hand on his cheek.

He put his hand on her hand, lifted it and kissed her palm. He picked up his menu. "So, what'll it be this time? The King Mackerel like before?" She looked at her menu. "No, there's a tuna special. I think I'll have that. What about you, Hon'?"

"I think I'll have the lobster stew. No fish for me. That trash really fouled my mood."

"Don't let it do that," and she knit her brows. "You have a lot more trenches you're going to encounter. Don't shut your mind off to them now. Keep it open and fresh."

"You're right," he backed up in his chair and folded his arms. "I just can't tell you what it did to me to see it, though."

"I think I know. What say we don't mention it again and enjoy our meal?"

He looked down for a minute. Then, looked up into her eyes. "You got it, Babe."

When they arrived home that night, Heather looked like she had something on her mind that she was nervous to share with him.

"That's okay, Babe." Victor removed his jacket. He seldom-to-never wore a tie of any sort, just starched white shirts so his collar stood up nice and straight. "Let's talk about it now. We need to get to bed to be on the boat at 6:00."

"Well, I can't rush through this," she said as she took off her scarf and ran her hands over back of the couch. "I know about the trouble you had with Monika."

"What's my first wife got to do with us?"

"Plenty, since it ended in divorce."

"Well, we aren't even married."

"Yet."

"So, that's what it is. You want to get married?"

"I think it's only right before the baby comes."

You could have bowled Victor over with that news.

"Baby? I thought you were on birth control pills," he said, incredulously.

"I am. But you know even those things aren't fool proof." She took her shoes off and worked her way to their bed room.

Victor was so shook up he hadn't taken another thing off.

"Look," she said. "It might be just what we need, a kind of glue that keeps us together. We don't know how we'll react to the little thing yet. Just give it a chance. Besides, we have nine months to get used to the idea. And, hey, it just might be the high light of your life."

Heather crawled into bed, negligee on, and said, "You'd better catch some Zzzs before that alarm goes off." Then, she turned her light off on the bedside table.

The next day they all met in the Sonar Mapping Room again to examine the floor and the tectonic plates at the bottom of the Mariana Trench, named for the Mariana archipelago. This was a very complicated trench compared to the Puerto Rico. It was located in the Pacific Ocean just south of Japan. For example, it had pretty much of mud volcanos. Its subduction zones, points where two plates collide, made it the longest and deepest trench on earth. It was designated a US monument in 2009. In 1997 the Challenger Deep, a British sub, had measured the depth of the trench near the south of Guam as 35,463 feet deep.

That would be the trench Victor was going to examine that day –solo. No one dared tell Heather. If they knew she was with child that would be all the more reason not to tell her. He could do this alone. He was well aware of the dangers, but he thought he had everything under control. That was Victor. Everything had to be under control, including his ex-wife, who had a lawsuit against him for his cruelty. He wondered what a baby would do to his career right now, except to stop for a ultrasound after the three-month period? And he was 56, by god! He needed to get that off his mind and focus on his present mission, especially since this was a solo deep dive. The radio buzzed with Patrick on the other side asking for a depth then a temperature reading. He responded with "2,023 and -20 degrees." Victor forgot was he was doing. He couldn't afford to do that anymore. His radio buzzed back on,

"Then you must be passing quickly through the twilight zone."

"Roger that," and Victor slipped on a thermal jacket.

"Let me know when you hit the midnight zone."

"Roger that one, too."

Suddenly, he heard a great bump and his little sub shuttered. He didn't know what that noise was, but it soon became apparent that he had no more electricity. It grew deathly cold in the sub, and he couldn't call up the crew on the radio. They all determined the freeze cut off the electricity, all they could do was sit and wait to see if it came back on, but they couldn't wait too long. Victor had put on a pull over cap, a pullover sweatshirt and a baklava and gloves. Finally, when he hit the Hadal Zone, though it was colder, the sub caught up with the temp, and the heater came back on. His radio, though through static, came back on as well. The Mariana Trench, seven miles deep, had only few new fauna: he saw a pink snailfish. and a whole slew of super giant antropods called amphipods, and a Dumbbo Octupus. The Dumbo is named after a character at Disney World that looks like Dumbo the Elephant. No human could survive outside the miniature sub in the Mariana Trench. The pressure wouldn't allow it. The pressure measured 16,000 pounds per square inch.

When the capsule called to come back up, Victor was hoping he wouldn't get dumped in the ocean again. The temperature in the Atlantic wasn't that bad, but he wasn't sure he could survive a dump in the Pacific. He knew that was the coldest ocean short of the Arctic. Hours later, once his miniature sub topped the choppy waters, the wind was blowing considerably. As usual, Heather and Hope were observing, until the cold weather chased them inside. He was glad. Though he didn't fall in the Pacific, she made him nervous each time she saw him when he was working.

When Victor parked his Tesla in the garage that evening, he told Heather he wanted to talk about her reaction to his jobs and how they made him nervous tonight. "Why can't you and Hope just stay in the mapping room?"

"Is that an order, Hon'?"

"Of course not, Babe."

"Well, it sure sounds like one to me."

"Oh, Heather, it's just that you make me nervous watching me."

"Well, that makes the two of us."

"Why didn't you tell me this from the beginning?"

"I wanted to make you proud of me," and at that, she hung her head.

Victor moved as close as he could get to her, given his Tesla's bucket seats, and took her in his arms. He whispered in her ear. "Oh, Heather there isn't a day I'm not proud of you." Then, he kissed her long and hard.

He went back to his seat.

"One more is the Java Trench…"

"Now don't bring that up. That's not fair. That's the most dangerous trench you could select. You know that's a Mauno Loa waiting to happen again, which could be any day now. Just ask Hawaii, or better yet, check the National Oceanic and Atmospheric Administration. The volcanos there have massive Tsunamis, as well."

"Look, I love you, Heather, but you're going to have to trust me to make my judgment calls. And, NOAA has nothing to do with my dives."

She said, "And I'm trying to give our baby a father." Then, she stepped out of the car and slammed the door.

It was a cold night in the house. Victor felt terrible about the argument, but it had to happen. Heather wanted to warm up to him, but felt it would soften her heart more than she wanted it to. When he rolled over toward her in bed, all the negativity went away, somehow, except she had to say it: and another thing, I don't want you going down alone again. He decided that was a small concession, so he just pulled her closer to him. They slept through the night in each other's arms.

The next day, at the boat launch, pretty much everyone seemed fresh after a good night's sleep. Patrick asked Victor if he had spoken to Heather about the Java Trench, and he got a cold stare about it. "I'll tell you during our next dive." He told him, which put the *Quaeritis* on the whole thing for now.

"You mean I'm going down with you? I thought it was to be another solo."

"Please don't let Heather hear you say that."

So Patrick started preparing the big boat for the trip around the Horn to the Pacific Ocean, and the crew and Victor started checking out the little sub. In time, Victor and Patrick headed to the Sonar Mapping Room to see what the ocean floor would like for him.

Victor pulled Heather out of the mapping room and asked her about "going down in the Philippine Sea, instead, in search of a WWII vessel no one has been able to find." He didn't bother to tell her that was because no one would go down that deep. It was in the Hadal Zone, but not as deep as the one they had just reached. As Victor had asked, and because it was such a fresh request, both Heather and Hope did not watch Victor surface.

Victor hated to be dishonest, but he hated more to be constrained. He said he'd have someone with him, but this time he'd pick his sonar specialist, Jeremie Morize, who had no mechanical experience. The name of the vessel was the USS Johnston (DD-557), nick named the Sammy B. It was on the floor some 21,181 feet down. Heather acquiesced, and she thanked Patrick for going down with him. He didn't say anything about Jeremie, even as Patrick looked at Victor. If Victor wanted her to know, he missed his chance to tell her.

So, they turned their boat southwest toward the Philippine Sea. You could hear Patrick cry, "All hands-on deck," which made Heather feel like she was in a real *Moby Dick* film. She loved the bumpy ride there, made even more bumpy by the size of the swells that grew from the day's chop. Then, quite suddenly, she leaned over the bow, and she retched.

Hmm, what's going on? Hope wondered, "You never said you felt bad before this boat ride. What's going on?"

"It just came over me quite suddenly."

"I could see that, and she pulled Heather's loose blouse tighter on her."

"You sure you don't have something hiding in there?"

Heather rolled her eyes. "Okay, but please keep this to yourself. I'm sure when Victor wants to tell the crew he'd like to tell you all together

"So, it *is* true. You guys are expecting." Hope didn't' know whether to congratulate her or pass her condolences. "So how did Victor take it? He seems like a career man to me."

"Oh, yes, he is very much a career man. I'm hoping the little tyke will change him."

"Hoping?"

"I know. I may be hoping against hope, but I do see cracks in his armor now and then."

Before too long the ship was hovering above the location of the Sammy B. By then, the little sub was all equipped and ready to drop. The water, however, was unruly and ready to squall. Victor had no patience for it; He had encountered that his whole life, and patience was one of his weaknesses. He swore, then asked Patrick, "if he were going down would this weather stop us?"

"Well, since you aren't taking a mechanic with you, it would give me reason for pause."

Victor looked at him for several minutes. There, there's my pause. Jeremie, he shouted, get your stuff and squeeze in.

It wasn't smart, but it was Victor. Just as soon as the tiny sub hit the water it was rocking, enough for Victor and Jeremie to lose their equilibrium.

"What's happening?" asked Jeremie/.

"Don't go on these missions much, do you?" Asked Victor.

"No, Sir. Don't get the chance."

"It's just something in your ears that doesn't like the rocking back and forth. It'll go away when we get below the waves."

After a few hours of squirming, Jeremie said, "Well, it's taking a long bloody time to get there."

"Just think of it as Christmas. Now we wait for what Santa is going to give us: new fauna. That's really exciting to me."

But, getting to the bottom gave them much more than that. After they reached the bottom of the Hadal zone, and the silt settled, they realized they nearly clipped the side of the Sammy B. They looked up amazed. Victor reached for his video recorder and started filming, talking as he filmed, they were the only ones to see this materialize before their eyes in person. Jeremie wanted to celebrate, but that exuberance was stamped out quickly when Victor did not. He radioed the crew above.

"Just a little, at least, by slapping backs,' Jeremie persisted.

Victor's transmission stated simply, "mission accomplished. Request permission to come aboard *immediately.*"

What was that? Patrick thought. *Victor never asked that before.* All the crew above them, except for Patrick, were grinning and high fiving when the little sub stopped dead in the Abysmal Zone.

"Something is wrong?" Said Patrick under his breath.

"Our sub is dead in the Abysmal Zone, and I'm afraid our ability to communicate won't be far behind."

"Wish we had more time to trouble shoot."

"Don't start in with me before I can get up there, now, damnit, you gotta get me out of…."

Patrick never heard the end of the sentence., never had a chance to. But the last thing he heard was the last transmission on the radio. He just tried to call Victor back, but it was dead. Victor and Jeremie's fate was in their hands now, and that's where it would stay.

So, Victor swore a mild oath, looked at Jeremie and said, "Well, I chose you for my second mate so here's the situation. You saw those boxes hanging off the Sammy B? Those were live depth charges, so we don't want to cause a whole bunch of swirls around them. It's a miracle we haven't already. About our predicament right now, I'm going to guess that the frigid water has caused a power shut down. It's happened before, but I don't have a mechanic in here to confirm it this time. I just know if we can't get the power back it'll eventually cut our O2 off. That'll be the end of us."

"And what can we do to keep that from happening?"

"I hate to tell you this, Kid, but we have to use up our emergency store of O2. And, as long as our transmitter is dead, I won't know anything else. It's not like we can crawl out of this sub with more than 13,000 feet per square inch squeezing us to death. If I were you, I'd be conserving my breath and my energy right now. Just look around and see if there is anything that may leap out at you besides that wrench right there; I'll be using it to open our reserve of six tanks we installed above for in that just such a thing has happened.

And with that, the minutes ticked away on the boat above. When Heather finally stepped out to check on the submersible's assent, she found Patrick on deck and is taken aback. "What in the world is going on, Patrick?"

"I hate it when he puts me in the middle of you two," Patrick says.

"Has he done that?" she asks.

"He sure has. He took a young sonar technician with him instead of me."

"Well, I wouldn't have approved of that at all."

"I think that's the problem. He's seeing what he can get away with. You just wait 'til he comes back up here."

"*If* he comes back up here. He's got himself in quite a jam now. I wouldn't be too hard on him. This back and forth has got to end with one of you *now.*"

All they could do was wait. Hours went by, but it would take hours for the little sub to come up or go down on its own. Thing was they wouldn't know the time it started.

When it became dark out, the crew and Heather all grew really despondent. *My child may grow up without a father after all.* She stepped inside, but she didn't give up watching for him.

Meanwhile, Patrick was aft in the boat scanning the water with lighted binoculars. He never gave up, no matter how late in the night it was. Then about a quarter to midnight, the little sub finally popped up to the surface on its own. Patrick's shout went out to everyone with, "all hands-on deck!" That was the sweetest call that Heather ever heard.

Men were throwing their jackets on and such; Hope and Heather were the only two completely dressed. The crewmen looked at Patrick to point them to the location. Two crewmen jumped into the ICB-1 rubber rescue boat and hurried to the sub, not knowing how much O2 they had left. When they got to it, they cleated it, then opened the hatch; both men were lethargic. They had to be pulled out one by one. Patrick shouted, "Give 'em oxygen soon as you can!" So, oxygen masks clung to both faces as they were brought on board.

"I knew when you asked my permission to come on board, something was very wrong," said Patrick.

Victor couldn't say anything; with the hatch open both men drew big breaths of very salty air: nectar of the gods. When they were brought aboard the big boat, and were still on oxygen, Heather came over to Victor and put her arms around him. "We didn't know if we'd ever see you alive again."

When he finally had his breath, he answered her. "I know, Babe, and I'm really sorry. I didn't know if we'd make it either."

Then Patrick asked, "well why did you ask for permission to come aboard *immediately?*"

Victor looked at Heather as if he wanted her to go somewhere else. But Patrick put his foot down. "No, Victor, all this deception has to stop now. I can't be a part of it anymore."

"Well. I'd rather not have Heather know this."

"And why is that. Victor?"

"Because I think it will affect all my dives from here on out."

"Not if Patrick goes with you." Offered Heather.

"And how would Patrick help me to know our sub would land just three feet from three live depth charges?

The day after the next day, Heather had an appointment for her trimester ultra sound. She was both excited and nervous.

"What you're nervous about, Babe? I'm nervous about what you may want. We haven't talked at all about it. That's probably because I don't have any druthers. And he chuckled. Like you, I just want a healthy baby. That's all."

"Oh. I'm so glad to hear that."

"Then, I guess we should at have shared that with each other. Wasn't any sense in you worrying in the least about that."

The nurse came in and asked, "Who's going first?"

They both laughed. That lightened the mood a bit.

The End

Kristen's
Chicken
Tractor

Kristen's Chicken Tractor

There is one person in my family who took after me and my dad: it is my niece, Kristen. My only niece, and, if you rolled the dice, you'd have a one and seven chances to get a girl. So, for her to take after me, is not only surprising; it's something I stumble over every day. That part of my family, I'm used to not hearing from. Josh seems to be a recluse by living in another state with just his girlfriends, and Kristen lives on a farm with boyfriends; her two children get shuttled about from their dad, and then to grandparents. She lives on some farm property. somewhere around Louisville, Kentucky.

I experienced the pains of suffering through walking out to discover dead chickens killed by my neighbor's dog, or by some foxes, or by some wild dogs, or whatever. What I did about it made the difference. I eventually asked Bob Gallloway to help me build them a run so I didn't have to deal with death constantly. After all, I was still teaching.

I got the materials, and we went from there. The expense was in the 3X6 boards; the fencing was little to nothing. The rest was a piece of cake. It literally was, because Bob and I are best friends. He helped me get that up in a day. It was fun, and I knew I'd be changing my chickens' lives for the better from there on out. That was right before I found out we'd be moving to Canyon Lake. Then it became sad. Very sad. You may say that I had a choice in the matter. You don't when it comes to money, and the other party had the money, Anyway, I should have managed my life better. You're right there. I changed that when we bought the property in Canyon Lake.

Still, I left Seguin having learned something. I had the knowledge. The **What to Do**, if you will. And, for once, I had something to do with it. Well, I can't go on Kristen's property, and build her a chicken house and a run, but I could get my brother, Greg, to go in with me half-sies, and have someone build her a chicken tractor.

So, reg and I scoped out the chicken tractors in his part of Louisville, and got it at both a decent price with just the perfect sturdiness to boot. The way it works is like this: with wheels on the back, you must move the tractor at night when the chickens are at roost. You want to move it to fresh grass where they will find new bugs and such. Then you move the water, the oyster shell and the feed back where it was under the roosting rods before night falls. I have no idea if Kristen has a rooster in this lot of chickens, but if she does, she wants to move it before he crows in the morning. The roosting rods are placed at the top in the dark rectangle, long with the laying stalls,

I do know that after the first night Kristen had her first egg. It was a green one so at least a part Aracuna laid it. After that it's a matter of policing their squabbling over bugs, laying stalls or positions on the roosting rods. Or just let them establish a pecking order which they will do on their own. They'll encounter a peck or two, but that never killed a chicken.

I asked her to send me the breeds she had, the colors of the chickens and the sexes, but I got nothing. I know she is a busy, working girl. but I guess I needed to ask more than I did. I will put the story in my book to entice her away from her job. Well, anyway, Proud Mama is pretty much the boss of every other chicken in the tractor by now. She has made it her business to claim the highest rung of the roost and the softest laying stall of the lot. As far as feed, oyster shell and water, there is nothing to fight over so, the only thing that they bicker about is who gets the biggest bug of the ones they find. Even there isn't much for her to challenge, since they usually give it to her if they see her coming.

She has become the beacon of where the tractor should be moved the next day; she steps to the side of the tractor and stares at the grass on that side. The very place she wants to hunt for bugs in a few hours. The others go along with her, of course. I mean she laid the first egg of the brood. She's Proud Mama, and no one will question that. Margot and JR watch her and will move the tractor at night where she wants it moved.

The End

About the Author

Peggy Marceaux

Peggy Marceaux is a retired English teacher who lives in Canyon Lake, Texas. She earned her Bachelor's Degree from Lamar University and her Masters of Arts from the University of Houston, where she specialized in British Literature.

Ms. Marceaux taught for 32 years; 11 in the Alvin Independent School District and 15 in the Comal Independent School District in TX, Chairing the High School English Departments in both.

Having raised chickens for twenty years, she loved the diversity among the breeds. This inspired "BeakSpeak", a story designed to help young people accept their differences and build confidence, through speech validation. Ever the English teacher, Ms. Marceaux believes the earlier you teach children language precision, the better it will help them succeed in their future relationships and careers.

Along with BeakSpeak, Ms. Marceaux is also involved with CLAW the Canyon Lake Area Writers at the Tye Preston Memorial Library in Canyon Lake, Texas where they meet for two hours the first and third Tuesday of each month. They enjoy letting their creative juices flow with writing prompts, have visiting speakers import helpful knowledge, and submit their 5,000-to-8,000-word short stories to Raconteur in the hopes of gaining publicity.

Short Story Collections:

About BeakSpeak - the Characters

The BeakSpeak characters are inspired from Peggy's own chickens! Some 30+ years ago Peggy began raising chickens on her farm and discovered that chickens have personalities. Along with their very personable characteristics they must learn quickly that there is a pecking order. Like human society, some chickens behave aggressively, others passively, and weak birds cannot survive a bully without a human intervening.

Her chicken coop, then became the English classroom, where Ms. Marceaux taught language skills for 32 years in high school. "My greatest reward was watching my students grow to respect one another, find their confidence, learn how to rationally think about the world around them, and then shape their views to fit in that world. I was able to help them do all this by teaching them that, when you think, speak and write precisely and concisely, using the clearest and most effective words, with the most energetic verbs to defend your views, the better you communicate your meaning."

The first BeakSpeak book is a colorful rendition of a classroom of chickens who are learning about thinking and language skills. Add to those techniques, Marceaux stimulates thought with her exploratory questions, and suggested answers. BeakSpeak, A Fable and Language Workbook is a perfect companion piece with this book as everyone can benefit from learning how to better communicate with others!

These books are available on Amazon. Learn more at

www.PeggyMarceaux.com